SALVATION

A Bradshaw Brothers Novel, Book Two

BILLIE PARSONS

Parsons Publishing LLC

This is a work of fiction. Names, places, incidents and situations resembling reality are purely coincidental and part of the authors imagination.

Cover design: Kristi Leigh at Vanilla Lily Designs
Editing: Amy Briggs

Parsons Publishing LLC

For my little brother.
Thank you for always inspiring me to be my very best, and for
always pushing me to try new things.
I cannot imagine growing up without you.

Chapter One

SAMANTHA

I sit and watch my best friend dance with her new husband, and I cannot help but be envious. She has gone through so much in the last year and she deserves the absolute best but sometimes she forgets that Ally and I exist. It is now that I make a vow to myself, I will not get lost in someone. I will not forget my roots. I will not forget my friends.

Jackson's older, brooding, brother walks up to me.

"Want to dance Sammy?" Maxwell asks.

I shake my head in annoyance as I take his hand to dance. Maxwell knows that I hate being called Sammy or Sam. My name is Samantha, what is so hard about that? He loves to push my buttons. Ever since Emma and Jackson had a dinner party all those months ago, Maxwell and I have developed this strange friendship. The kind where he gets too intoxicated to call a cab so instead, he calls me, or when he cannot get a woman to leave his house, he calls me. Where if I need someone to talk to, but he is too drunk to remember the next day, but we talk anyway. Yeah, super healthy relationship.

He pulls me close to him as we reach the dance floor and I can smell the whiskey on his breath. His hand is lower than it should be on my back, so I reach around and push it up. He huffs out his breath against my ear and lowers his hand again.

"Maxwell. You're drunk. Maybe I should take you home," I say.

"I'll take you home," he whispers huskily.

"Yeah. Right. Let's go."

MAXWELL

I SEE DARKNESS AND MY HEAD FEELS LIGHTER THAN IT should. I can feel someone tugging my shoes off and I try and sit up to see who it is.

"Stay laying down Maxwell. You are extremely intoxicated. And you need to go to bed," Samantha says with her wonderful, watered-down southern drawl.

"Oh, Sammy! Come to bed, won't you?" I ask.

"Go to sleep Max," she barks.

I wake the next morning with a glass of water and Tylenol on my nightstand. I can still smell Samantha's perfume in the room, but she is gone.

SAMANTHA

FIVE MONTHS LATER

I SIT ON THE COUCH WHEN ALLISON, BETTER KNOWN AS Ally, my best friend and roommate, finally comes out of the bathroom.

"Morning," Ally yells from the kitchen. I just grunt in response. "Crap. What's wrong?"

"Nothing. Everything," I moan into the couch pillows. She comes and sets a cup of coffee in front of me on the table and sits next to me and reaches for the television remote.

"All right then. I have about twenty minutes before I need to leave for class. You can either talk or I'll watch the news," Ally says.

Pushing myself to sit upright, I pull my legs underneath me, slump my shoulders forward and sigh before starting. "I care too much."

"Are we talking about something or someone in particular?" I shoot her my best bitch glare. "So, Max then."

"Why do I keep answering his fucking calls? He is tearing me apart. Ally... he is drinking a lot." I turn to face her and emphasis, "A lot, a lot. Last night when he called me, I could barely understand him, and some guy grabbed his phone and gave me an address in the south end of town and hung up. I was so scared to go get him. These big thug-like guys threw him out of the house and he hardly made it to the car before he was puking and passing out."

Ally puts her hand on my knee, "Have you talked to Jackson at all? He might be able to help."

"Their baby is due soon. I don't want to bother him with this too," I admit.

"It's his brother. Call Jackson, or at least Uncle J," Ally says as she gets up to leave. Before she walks out the door of our apartment, she looks back at me. "You need to put your foot down. Stop answering him if you have to," then she walks out as if that is so easy.

My feelings for Maxwell are so complicated. Some days I think that I love him and other days I want nothing to do with him. On those not so loving days I still, for some reason, care about what he is doing, how he is and whether he is thinking about me. My inner soul calls out for his but my brain battles against my soul, saying no more of this shit.

Knowing that she is right I reluctantly reach for my cell phone and text Jackson to see if we can meet for lunch.

"HEY, SAMANTHA. HOW ARE YOU?" JACKSON SAYS AS HE approaches. He pulls me into a hug and gestures for me to sit across from him. "Your text has me a bit concerned. You said that you wanted this to stay between us." He leans forward slightly. "Are you ok?"

"You're too kind, Jackson. I am fine." I don't know how to tell him that I think that his brother is an alcoholic, so I fidget with the menu for a brief moment to try and gather my thoughts. "It's about Max actually."

"What about him?" Jackson asks.

I sit up a little taller. "Look I don't know how to say this, so I am just going to put it out there." I pause while the waitress refills our water. "I think Max is...an alcoholic," I whisper.

"I was afraid of this. Emma and I have had our suspicions, but nothing definite." Hearing that others, his family, are concerned as well soothes my heart in some twisted and dark way. I shouldn't be relieved that other people think that he has a drinking problem, but it makes me feel like I am not losing my mind. "Has he called you, did he reach out, Samantha."

I shake my head. "No, not exactly."

"Please cut the shit, Samantha. I don't mean to be harsh, but this is my brother," Jackson barks, his worry for his brother evident in the harshness of his words.

"Look. I didn't want to worry you or Emma, so I have kept it to myself for some time. Max and I."

"Are what? Dating? Fucking?"

I put my hand up to stop him. "If you would let me finish... Max and I have what some might call a toxic relationship. We are not dating, or fucking for that matter. He gets super drunk and calls me to save his ass and some-times I call him because I know whatever I tell him, he will forget about the next day. I know you are going to say that it's not healthy, but I already know."

"Okay, then. You have probably seen a lot. If you want to block his number, I can compensate you for your help."

Hurt and frustration lace my word, "That is not why I told you, Jackson! I told you because I don't want him to die!" I stand up from the table and storm away from him. Typical billionaire, throwing his money around like it is nothing. I sit in my car, collecting my thoughts when Jackson taps on the window. I roll it down enough to hear him.

"Sorry...I...I'll talk to him," is all he says before he walks back to the café. I roll my window back up and drive to work.

Chapter Three

MAXWELL

POUNDING ON THE DOOR WAKES ME UP FROM A GLORIOUS dream about a southern blonde goddess. I roll out of bed and now the pounding in my head starts. The world tilts on its axis but the pounding on the door doesn't stop.

"Okay. Okay. I'm coming!" I yell. I open the door to see my little brother and his very pregnant wife standing at the door. "To what do I owe the pleasure of a visit this morning."

Jackson pushes inside. "It's three in the afternoon."

Emma pats my arm in an affectionate, motherly way. "Hey, Max."

"All right. What can I do for you guys?" I try and hold back the vomit that keeps creeping up my throat.

Both of them head to the dining room and Jackson stands behind a chair that Emma eases herself into. "Sit down Maxwell," Jackson says coldly.

I sit and fold my hands on my lap waiting for him to lay into me.

"You have a problem," he starts.

"Geez, Jackson," Emma interrupts, "Max, we are worried about you. Not just me and your brother. Everyone. We know that you have been drinking a lot more lately."

"Is this some type of intervention? 'Cause you don't know what you—"

"What we are talking about? Seriously. I can see the sweat on your brow, Max, it isn't hot in here. You look like you are about to blow chunks. You have to remember my wife had some serious morning sickness I know the look," Jackson says.

"I ate something that upset my stomach," I lie.

"Bullshit! I know you put your hands under the table to hide the shakes. You think we don't see it, but we do." Jackson starts to pace the dining room. "Samantha told me that you have been calling her almost every night to get home."

"Get out," I say.

"What?" they both question in unison.

"Get the fuck out of my house!" I start to yell.

Kicking them out of the house is the only option I have at the moment. They don't know what I am going through. They don't see my pain. I know that they see me drink but that is just the tip of the iceberg.

Knowing that I cannot change their perceptions of me I pour myself a fresh glass of scotch.

Chapter Four

SAMANTHA

MAX HASN'T CALLED OR TEXTED ME IN ALMOST TWO weeks. It is strange not having him need me. Every night I wake to every little noise thinking that it is him trying to get a hold of me. Jackson texted me to tell me that Emma had their baby and asked if I had heard from Max. Seems that he hasn't really talked to anyone.

I sit in the elevator that will take me to Max's apartment and as I watch the numbers flash at the top of the panel I try and figure out what I'm going to say to him. If he is home, do I ask if he is okay? What if he isn't alone? My thoughts halt when I step out of the elevator and see two very large men dressed in dark jeans and dress shirts, standing outside Max's door.

I approach cautiously. "Hi. Can I help you?"

"We are looking for Maxwell," the smaller of the two men say.

"Who are you?" I ask nicely.

The bigger man steps up very close to me and twirls a

strand of my hair. He smells of liquor, cigars, and expensive cologne. After everything that happened to Emma last year, I know not to let my fear show, so I stand as still as possible and wait for him to move away or say something. I feel his breath on my cheek when he fists my hair and inhales my scent before he takes a couple of steps back. "Baby girl, you must be Sammy. My name Raymundo Sands but you can call me Boss. This is Ace." He gestures to the other man.

"How do—" I start.

"Just tell Mr. Bradshaw that we were here," Ace says before they push past me.

I shake my head clear and walk to Max's door. I know they had already knocked and did not get an answer, so I reach into my purse and pull out a receipt and a pen and write on the back.

Max,
> *Please call me.*
> *XOXO Samantha*

I don't hear from him though. Nothing but radio silence.

My cell phone dings as I sit at my desk and my heart does a little flip each time it goes off in the hopes that its him. My heart breaks all over again when I see that it is just my mother asking me to call her this evening.

I wake up in the middle of the night to get a glass of

water and see that I have a text message from an unknown number.

Max: Don't worry about me. I am OK.

I try and call the number, but a connection is never made. I lay awake in bed until I see the sunshine peeking in under my curtains. My cell phone starts to ring then.

"Max?" I answer.

"Who is Max honey?" my mother says on the other end.

Sitting up in bed, "Sorry mom. I thought it was someone else."

IT HAS BEEN A FEW DAYS SINCE MAX TEXTED ME AND I have decided to silence my phone in the hopes of finally getting some sleep. Knowing it's silenced allows me to not obsess over every vibration and noise that goes off when one of the girls texts me or my social media apps send a notification. Ally barges in my room "Samantha. Phone call for you."

"What?" I ask sleepily. She thrusts her phone at me. "Hello?"

"Sammy babe!" Max yells into the phone. "Where are you? I'm so sorry. Please come home."

"What the hell Max? You aren't making sense."

"Please. I know I've messed up. Just please come home." He mutters before he hangs up.

I give the phone back to Ally and I get up and throw on a pair of sweatpants over my underwear I was sleeping in and leave my tank top as is.

"Are you seriously going over there?" Ally asks.

I turn to face her as I slip on my tennis shoes. "Yeah. He wasn't making sense. I want to make sure he is okay." I walk past her and out the front door quickly.

Riding in the familiar elevator to a familiar apartment with a stranger inside in eerie. That is what Max has become, a stranger. I have had a lot of time to think about what I truly know about Max, which isn't much, I start to daydream.

"Max, you are too much. How am I supposed to ever tell anyone my secrets if you've already heard them?" I say into the phone.

"They aren't really secrets then, are they?" Max replies.

"How is it that you have heard almost everything about me, and I know hardly anything about you?" I ask.

Max lets out a deep breath and starts, "Well Sammy, what do you want to know about me, I have many secrets."

My daydream is interrupted by the ding of the elevator telling me I have reached my destination. I reluctantly walk to his apartment, but I don't bother knocking before I turn the handle and walk inside. The living room is covered in women's clothing and vodka bottles. The dining room table is covered in takeout boxes and white powder covers a small reflective surface. I walk towards his room, bile rising in my throat.

"Max?" I yell down the hallway. I hear screeching and

giggling coming from his room, but I don't enter. I have seen this a lot of times with him. He calls just to have me help him get the girls out and to clean his place.

"Sammy! Come in babe!" Max hollers through the door. I push the door open and the scene in front of me makes me want to puke even more. Clothes are thrown about, empty bottles laying around, two girls laying naked in his bed making out, while he sits in only his boxers in a chair that was moved from the living room, glass in hand. Needles, spoons, and an excess of lighters lay around, as well as sex toys, dildos, a strap-on, and a bottle of lube. . Before, when I played the role of savior, it wasn't this bad. So, when I start to talk, I stop myself and try again, not letting all my anger and fear out at once.

"Get out of my house!" I yell at the women. They don't seem to even notice me, so I walk up to the bed and my fury is released, I grab a hold of one of the girl's hair and pull her head towards me. "Did I stutter?" The woman I grab stares at me in horror when she realizes I am not here to join their party, but to break it up. I push her away from me and both the girls quickly jump from the bed and grab clothes as they run out. I walk up to Max and pull the empty glass from his hand, "Go take a shower."

While Max is in the bathroom, I get to work in his room, stripping and remaking the bed with fresh linen, cleaning up all the bottles and paraphernalia. I throw all the clothes in a trash bag, I'm not trying to figure out whose clothes are whose. Max walks from the bathroom with only a towel around his waist and sits on the edge of his bed. "Samantha...I—" he starts.

I out a hand up to stop him, "You're what? Sorry?

Enough Maxwell. You cannot keep doing this. I can't keep saving you."

"I never asked you to save me, Samantha."

"Really? What was this then?" I ask. "Listen Max you need to get some help. I am leaving in a few days. Christmas is in a week, and I am going to see my parents. Jackson and Emma just had their baby, and Uncle J is out of town. No one will be here to save you next time. What are you going to do if no one is around to answer your calls?" He shrugs his shoulders in indifference. "This is what I'm talking about Max. If you don't care what happens then why are you bringing me and everyone else into the shit storm you have created?

Max gets up and walks over to me and wraps his arms around me. He doesn't say anything, but I hope what I said got through to him this time.

Max is asleep when I finish cleaning his apartment and head back to my own home. I left a note for him.

Save yourself.
XOXO

Chapter Five

MAXWELL

I FUCKED UP.

I fold Samantha's note and put it in my wallet as I leave the house.

This is my fifth time going to rehab. This time I am telling people. This time I will try harder.

Jackson pulls up to the outside of the Canadian rehab center I chose, and we sit in the car for a moment.

"I am proud of you Max," Jackson says.

"I *will* do this," I reply.

He leans over the center console and hugs me with one arm, "I love you brother." I don't answer him. I can't, not now. I get out of the car and grab my bag from the backseat before I head inside.

As someone who has seen many rehab centers, this one is just like the rest. Over the top with the AA and NA logos, prayer groups happening off in the yard. I walk to the front desk, "I am checking in, I have an appointment."

"What's your name, sir?" the front desk lady asks.

"Maxwell. Maxwell Bradshaw."

"Hang out for a moment and someone will come get you."

Ten minutes later, two men walk out in dark blue scrubs, "Maxwell?"

"Max is good." I stand and shake their hands.

"Welcome to Helping Futures. We are glad you are here. Please follow us."

I follow them, knowing what the next thirty days has in store for me, and not knowing what the next thirty will do to Samantha. She left for her parent's house last night and I decided not to tell her I was doing this. Not in the fear that she would be upset, but in the fear that if I screw this up, she will never forgive me. Something about Samantha makes me believe in myself and the future. She makes me want to be better. I cannot keep hurting her the way I have been, she deserves so much more than that.

ADMITTING TO A BUNCH OF STRANGERS ALL THE BAD things you have done is much harder than most people would think. Telling the nurses all the alcohol and drugs I have been using when no one else knows. Confiding in my counselor and ignoring my ego long enough to tell him that I was stealing money from my brother and I's company to pay for the drugs because I lost a lot of my fortune gambling. Asking these strangers not to judge and ridicule me anymore than I already have when I tell them that I continue to hurt the woman who cares about me the most because I am afraid she will reject me when she finds out the truth about everything I have done. These strangers, who have seen their own share of hell, but still listen to me talk about how I refused to cope when my parents died and when Jackson and Emma were both hurt last year. How I ignored my fear and drank away my worries scares me because no one else seems to have understood me in the past when I tried talking about it. Confessing that I forgot how to have fun without cocaine, how watching people use would turn me on. How the first time I tried Heroin, I felt like I could take on the world. Allowing myself to be vulnerable in all ways, I tell these people how I would hide my track marks on my arms when I converted in needle use. Letting people see me in a way that I never admitted to before, scares the living shit out of me, but I know that for this to work. I have to.

Chapter Six

SAMANTHA

LEAVING MY PARENT'S HOUSE AND COMING BACK TO
Seattle is hard. Ever since the girls and I moved out here I
have wanted to go back home. Something about Georgia
feels natural to me. I was born and raised in Georgia so
that might be why Seattle has never felt like home to me.

"I'm so glad you are back. It was getting lonely around
here." Ally says in a way of greeting me.

"Hey, Ally," I say as I hug her. "How is everything, and
everyone?"

"Good." Ally leads me to the kitchen and pours us both
a cup of coffee. "You have got to see the baby, he is getting
so big already. Emma said that she was tiny as a baby so the
big boy genes must come from Jackson. Uncle J is still
gone, and Jackson said he is off taking care of business."

"Max?" I ask.

"Not sure. I haven't heard from him since before you
left. He wasn't at Jackson and Emma's for New Year's
either. I'm sure he will pop up."

"I'm going to go unpack then. If you don't have a class tonight, I want to run something past you."

"Sure. I can order Thai and we can stay in tonight."

"Yeah. Sounds good. Thanks, Ally."

I shove my suitcase in my closet, not bothering to unpack, and for the first time since before I left, I text Max.

Me: Hey. Back in town. You doing OK?

I don't want to fixate on whether or not he will text back, so I decide to shower and take a nap before dinner with Ally later.

When I wake up, it is early evening, not yet time to eat, and since I put in my notice at my job before I left, I have no work to do. I really wasn't happy with the work I was doing anyway and I think subconsciously I was already making my decision to leave Seattle permanently. Telling my best friend that I want to change my entire life around at twenty-six years old seems like a quarter-life crisis. Hell, maybe that is what is happening.

Ally knocks on my door an hour later and I put my laptop to the side to answer. "Take out is here," she says lifting a hefty bag full of food.

We eat in silence for a few minutes before I ask her about school. Ally is a law student, top of her class, book nerd type student so if anyone ever wants to change the subject, ask Ally about school. She rattles on about how she is glad that this is the last term before her internship applications go out and about the cute professor that is teaching her Criminal Thinking class.

"Hey. Did you ask me about school in order to not tell me what is going on with you?" Ally asks.

"Maybe." I avoid eye contact and stir my noodles again.

"Samantha. What's up?" she asks hesitantly.

I glance up at my friend, I am so proud of her, and seeing her face soften when she realizes I am having a hard time, makes a tear slip down my cheek. I whip it away and start, "I quit my job before I left. I told my parents I want to come back to Georgia, and they said that they want me home too. But, leaving you. Leaving Emma? This is really hard for me."

"Leaving Max will be harder," Ally adds.

"What?"

"I support your decision, no matter what it is. I might not like that my best friend is leaving, but you are going home. My dad still lives there so I'll come visit. You can come here anytime. But I think that if you leave Max here, that is what will hurt you the most."

"He doesn't answer my calls or texts half the time. He is using me, Ally. I can't keep this up," I confess.

Ally reaches across the table and puts a hand on my arm as she says, "It still hurts though."

I lose it then. Tears flow freely and I have a hard time catching my breath. She's right. Part of me cares deeply for Max, the other part of me loathes him. My heart and my brain are telling me to do two different things and I feel as though either way I am going to get hurt.

After I have calmed down, some Ally starts to talk again. "Let's finish eating, watch a movie, and tomorrow we can go to Jackson and Emma's and we can tell them what is going on." I nod my head in agreement.

EMMA LOVES THE IDEA OF ME AND ALLY COMING OVER, so much so she says that it is another family dinner party, like the one all those months ago when I first met Max. We walk into their house and I am assaulted by the smell of home-cooked southern food Emma must be cooking. Other than her being a kickass mom, wife, friend, and nurse, she is one hell of a cook. The aroma of the food makes me feel that much better about my decision to leave. Not only is my heart saying I should go back south but so is my stomach, and while I promised Ally I'd stay until our lease is up in four months, I know that once it is, I will go back home.

Jackson peeks around the corner, baby Christopher in his arms. "Hey ladies. Everyone is in here." Ally and I head his way. When we enter the dining and kitchen area, literally everyone is there. Uncle J sits at the island talking to Jackson as he sits back down. Lincoln, Max's friend, sits at the table talking to Granny and Charles, Emma stirs the food on the stove, and then there's Max. Fucking Max, stands next to her laughing at something she said. I stop in my tracks for just a moment when Ally nudges me and whispers, "Who's that guy with Granny and Charles?"

"That's Linc. Let me introduce you?" I smirk.

"Hey sorry to interrupt. Lincoln, this is Allison, she is my friend I was telling you about."

"Ally," she corrects.

"Allison is a beautiful name. Ally's good too. Most people call me Linc. I would like to say I have heard a lot about you but that would be a lie."

"Nice to meet you."

I leave them to converse, and Jackson hands me the baby. "Your hands are empty, and I need to help Emma." Sitting in the living room talking to a baby who doesn't understand what I am telling him is helping me sort my thoughts. Max comes and sits across from me, and he leans forward and rests his arms on his knees.

"Sammy?" I shoot him a glare for using the nickname, but I peek up again to see that he is clean shaven, his face looks fuller, his hair is cut, and he has a water bottle in his hands.

"Hi, Max."

"How are you? How was your trip?" he asks.

"Good." I get up and take sleeping Christopher and put him in the playpen. "Where were you, Max?" I turn back towards him and he grips the water bottle a little tighter. "Max? Are you ok?"

"I was taking care of some stuff. I'm fine," he answers. "Thank you for everything you have done for me, I asked for much more than I ever should have. I can't find all the right words to explain how grateful I am, Sammy. I want to make it up to you in whatever ways I can. Let me take you out on a date, it'll be mutually beneficial. You get good food, and a sober version of me, and I get to spend time with the most beautiful women I have ever met."

"Max, I—"

"I'm thirty-three days sober," he says showing me his thirty-day chip.

"I'm glad to hear that. But Max, that doesn't change everything that's happened," I explain.

"I know. Just think about it." Then he walks off to join the others again. He doesn't say anything about it again throughout the evening, but I definitely thought about it. It's hard to say no to him even though I know I will be leaving soon, and I would be leaving whatever our relationship turned into, if anything. At the end of dinner, I tell everyone my plans to leave. While everyone seemed to understand, no one really liked the idea, especially Max. He got irritated at the situation and tried to argue with me about it.

Before leaving Max stops me in the hallway. "Are you really leaving?"

"Yes. In about four months."

"I don't understand. How can you just leave?"

"It isn't that simple Max. You think I am making this decision on a whim. I'm not." He follows me out to the front porch. He watches me and paces back and forth like I'm going to change my mind because he wants me to. "None of this is easy Max. If you think that I am doing this to hurt you in some way, just know, it hurts me the same." Again, he watches me. I can tell that he is upset by my choices, but I have to do what is right for me and my future. Whether or not he is part of it.

"I thought about the date. I'll go but not until this weekend. Okay? But it doesn't change the fact that in a few months, I'm moving back home."

His smile stretches across his face, "Yeah, okay." It almost feels evil to have said yes to him, but I can't help saying yes. Even if only for the briefest of times I will be able to experience everything my heart has wanted from Max. .

Chapter Seven

MAXWELL

THESE LAST COUPLE OF DAYS HOME HAVE BEEN exhausting. Lincoln has been at my place nearly every day checking on me, Jackson calls almost every two hours. Being home isn't easy. I see people on the street that I used with, I walk by bars and can smell the alcohol. I get text messages from people asking me to help them get loaded. I thought about changing my number but getting all my business cards reprinted and everything is too much work. I talked to Jackson about going back to work next week, and he seems happy to have me back—even after I told him about the money. He was less upset about that than he was about me hurting our friends and family. My phone chimes in my pocket.

Boss: I heard you're back.

I don't respond. He is a huge trigger for me, hell he was my dealer, and I thought a friend, for a long time. I clearly was wrong.

After having dinner with Lincoln and his daughter, I get another message.

Boss: You still owe me Max.

I am pretty sure I will always owe him something, that is just the way Boss works his business, but I am not sure what he is talking about. I refuse to answer. It's too early in my sobriety.

Chapter Eight

SAMANTHA

I SHOULD HAVE KNOWN BETTER.

What else was I expecting, I know how he is. I knew that saying yes to Max would hurt me more than just saying no. I should not have listened when he said he was better. Max was supposed to pick me up for our date two hours ago. I send him probably ten text messages, calling him every name in the book. After the first one, he stopped reading them. My messages all say sent but not read. I call Lincoln to see if he knows anything, but he hasn't talked to Max since this morning. Having a big heart sucks, because now I have to go over to his place and make sure he is all right. *Why the hell do I do this?* I remind myself times like these are just another reason why I am moving. I never dealt with this bullshit before I came here.

I knock on Max's apartment door a couple of times, but when he doesn't answer I call his cell phone. I can hear it ringing inside, which is weird because he doesn't go anywhere without his phone. I try the handle, but it doesn't budge. I knock harder this time.

"Max! Are you in there?" I shout through the door. I don't hear a response but something in my gut is telling me to go in. Back when I was a teenager, I had this boyfriend that taught me all the illegal ways to get through a locked door. Lock picking being one of those, I pull the bobby pin from my bun to use and a pocketknife from my purse and after a couple of tries, the lock clicks open.

I walk through his place and am surprised to see everything seems pretty normal. I get to his bedroom realize that's not the case at all. His room is in disarray, clothes are spreading around, the bed is unmade, and an empty beer can sits on the dresser. I shake my head in disappointment and sadness for Max. I walk around the mess and make my way into the bathroom. Panic hits me like a freight train. I dial Linc's number, hit speakerphone, and drop the phone next to me as I check on Max.

"Hey," Linc answers.

"Linc. I need your help! Call Uncle J and get to Max's right now." I hope that the urgency in my voice gets through to him. Instead of having Max's name spread all over the news, *Billionaire Bradshaw Brother almost dies from drug overdose*. Calling for Joshua makes sense. He is a recently retired military surgeon, he saved Jackson and Emma last year, why not see if he can save this nephew.

"I'm with Jackson and Joshua now. We are on our way. What's going on Samantha, you're on speaker now." I can hear the tires screech on the road as their car changes directions.

"I...I don't know. Joshua, please tell me what to do." I

say with tears running down my cheeks, my hands shake as I touch Max's neck to feel for a pulse.

"Depends, what's going on?" Uncle J says calmly.

I hesitate with my words because to describe the scene in front of me will change everyone's opinion on Max. "We are in the bathroom. Umm...Max is passed out. He is laying in his puke. There is a needle on the floor next to a bottle of vodka, he has a belt. Oh my god. Joshua, I think he was shooting up drugs!" The panic in my voice increases.

"Listen to me, Samantha. Does he have a pulse?"

"Yeah, I checked his neck like you showed us. It's weak.

"Is he breathing okay?" Uncle J asks.

"Umm...well he is taking breaths, but they seem far apart."

"We are in the elevator now," Linc says. A few minutes later, all three of them are surrounding us in the bathroom. I try and back away, to get away from this scene but Joshua grabs my hand.

"He is going to need you for this."

I look at him, confusion is clearly written on my face. He directs the boys to sit Max up a bit and move him away from the puke, he kicks away the drugs and alcohol, and he removes the belt from Max's arm. He has me sit against the wall with Max straddled by my legs. "Wrap your arms across his chest like you are hugging him, and put your head next to his to hold it up." I try and do as Uncle J explains and he corrects my head location a little.

"Max! I need you to wake up for me bud!" Uncle J hollers at him. "I am going to give him something that will stop and reverse the overdose."

"What if you are wrong?" I ask.

"If I am wrong then nothing will change." He answers. He leans towards us and sticks an oddly shaped white tube-like thing, labeled as Narcan into Max's nose. "Now we wait and see if it works."

After only a few moments, Max starts to stir in my arms. "Max?"

He doesn't answer, instead he just turns to the side and starts to puke again. He stays in the slumped position and once he stops puking his breathing becomes slow again. Jackson reaches over and pulls Max back into the position he was before in my arms. Joshua reaches into his bag and pulls out two more of the containers and he administers them.

Seconds later, that feel like years, Max starts to fight me. He starts to push off of me, "What the hell?" he yells out. Once he realizes that I am the one he is fighting, he settles down some. He mutters curse words under his breath but nuzzles he face in my cleavage. "Sammy?" he asks.

I shush him and smooth back the black locks of hair that had fallen into his face. "I don't feel so great," Max gets out and leans across my lap before he starts to vomit all over again.

"This is normal," Uncle J tells us all.

Max starts to get up and I let him, the men move to help him, and he sits on the side on the bathtub. I quickly stand and move to the edge of the bathroom.

"I fucked up big-time guys," Maxwell says to the men in the room. He glares up at them with disappointment in his eyes. He scans the room and locks eyes with me. "You need to leave Samantha." The fact that he didn't call me Sammy burns almost as much as the words he did say. I know he was mad at me when I told him I was moving whether or not we go on our date but for him to push me away right now is not fair, but I decide to take this opportunity as an out. I think it's time to end our toxic relationship before it goes too far. I tell myself walking away right now will make my move that much easier. It will make moving on emotionally that much easier.

So, I do what any logical person should do. I walk out of his bathroom, out of his apartment, out of his building.

Out of his life.

Chapter Nine

MAXWELL

JACKSON SLAPS ME ON THE HEAD, "WELL THAT WAS THE stupidest fucking thing you could ever do."

"Really? Getting high after thirty-seven days instead of going on the date with that beautiful woman wasn't more stupid?" I ask sarcastically.

"No. Telling her to leave was the dumbest thing I think I have ever heard you say," Jackson says.

I sit up taller, rub my hands across my face and ask, "Do you think that after everything I have put her through she wants to see this. Experience this." I gesture around the room.

Jackson walks to the bathroom door, "She loves you. You are fucking asshole." Then he walks out, I don't hear the front door open or close, so I don't think he has left but he is not in the bathroom anymore. Linc and Uncle J mumble their agreements.

"What am I supposed to do, really?" I ask. I am

defeated. I let everyone down, I let myself down. I don't know how I can keep moving forward when all I do is fuck everything up.

"Let's get you to a meeting. Okay?" Linc suggests.

Chapter Ten

SAMANTHA

My emotions have been all over the place since Max asked me to leave so I have decided to turn them off. I did this a few times when I was a teenager and my parents thought I was losing my mind, but really it just makes things a little bit easier for me. I only have a short amount of time left here in Seattle, and I want to make the most of it. To start my not so healthy coping skills, I reach for my cell phone and redownload all the popular hookup apps. If I am not feeling my emotions, then I don't have to feel bad about sleeping around and going on dates.

I wouldn't say that I am off the charts sexy, but I know how to use my assets. The men on these sites notice it too. Within minutes of restarting my accounts and updating my location, I get a couple of matches. What harm can be done with me having some fun?

THREE WEEKS AND SIX GUYS LATER, I AM STARTING TO
feel even more dead inside. Which is almost my goal. I
don't really want to die but sometimes I envy the dead.
Not having to deal with all of the day to day drama and
bullshit of life. I roll over in bed and see that the guy from
the bar last night didn't leave. *Fucking great.* I laugh to
myself at the irony. Just a couple of months ago I was
helping Max get women out of his place and now I am
afraid to be rude to this guy who won't leave my place. A
knock on my door makes the guy next to me stir and I stay
quiet, hoping that Ally gets the point.

"Samantha?" Maxwell's voice echoes through my
bedroom door. It seems Ally did let him in. Of course, he
would come here now. I stay still and barely breathe as
though he can see me through the door and that if I make
myself small enough, just maybe I will disappear. I am not
that lucky though.

"I know you are in there. I'm not doing this through
the door so..." the door swings open and Max enters the
room. He stares at me, to the man next to me, then back at
me. His vision must go red because he stares at me, points
a finger at the man and turns his head to look at the man.
He walks up the side of the bed, tosses a T-shirt at me, and
throws the covers off my bed. The man next to me stirs
awake, he turns, and Max is on him. He grabs a hold of the
man's neck and pulls him up to face him. "I'm going to give
you about two seconds to get the fuck out of here before I
beat the shit out of you."

"Woah man. Your girl said she was single. I didn't
know," the man says clawing at Max's grip. Max drops the
guy and he runs out as fast as he can after grabbing his

clothes. He doesn't even have shoes on when he slams the front door closed.

"What the fuck Max?" I ask.

He storms towards me and gets soclose to me that I can almost count the hairs that have started to grow on his chin before he stops, takes a deep breath, and steps back, hands fisted at his sides. "Who the fuck was that?"

"It doesn't matter Max. What are you doing here?"

Looking down at the floor he says, "He isn't good enough for you."

Completely frustrated I blurt, "And what, *you* are?" I regret almost instantly that I said it, but I stand behind my words. Max thinks that he can control my life and that is not the case. Maybe throwing some of my pain back at him will get his attention.

Max doesn't respond right away. Instead, he looks up at me as if to make sure I am really the one who said that. He looks me in the eye and says, "No Sammy, I am not good enough either," before he turns and walks out of the room.

I know what I said hurt him, but damn it, I have had enough. He doesn't get to treat me like shit and walk all over me then show up here and expect things to be normal.

A little while later, I walk out and Ally hands me an envelope. "He asked me to give this to you."

I open the envelope and in it is a note on the back of an old receipt, like the one I left him.

Sammy

I am going back to rehab today. I'm sorry for everything.

XOXO Max

The wall I built against my emotions breaks, I sink to the floor, and tears stream down my face. Ally checks over my shoulder at the note and sits on the floor with me while I cry it out.

For whatever reason, the moment things start to seem good for me, something about Max forces me to start over.

I look at the envelope again and inside is a key with a note attached to it.

It's for the apartment. Just in case.

In case of what. In case he is overdosing in the bathroom again, in case he needs help kicking people out. Anger fuels me and my tears dry quickly. I need to give this key back because I will not find the man I love in his own puke like that ever again.

WHEN I FINALLY GET TO HIS APARTMENT, I POUND ON the door a few times with no answer. I refuse to use the key he gave me, so I slide it under the door to his space. I wait around for five minutes, knocking occasionally. He doesn't answer. I lean against the door and slide down it. My anger has subsided, and I know that Max isn't in this apartment, he is on his way to rehab, trying to better himself.

I don't know how long I sit there thinking about everything we did, everything we could have had. Hours, I think. A familiar man walks up to me and crouches next to me. "Hey, baby girl." I watch him for a moment, trying to place his face.

He studies me for a moment. "Boss," he reminds me.

"Maxwell isn't here," I tell him.

He places a hand on my knee and leans in a bit, "Do you know how I can find him?" I shake my head no, and it is the truth. I don't know where he is, how to call him, or anything. "Well isn't that a bummer." Boss takes a deep breath and stands up, and reaches his hand out to me. "Come now baby girl, he has some debt to pay off."

I had already grabbed his hand when he said that, "What is that supposed to mean? I don't have the money to pay you." He doesn't release my hand and just laughs at my words.

"That is not what I mean. You can work to pay it off." I try and pull my hand free, but Boss tightens his grip.

"I don't understand," I admit.

Boss pulls me into the elevator and once we start to move, he pushes the stop button, and the whole elevator jerks at the sudden change. Boss lets go of me only long enough to place a hand around my throat and he pushes me up against the mirrored wall. "Listen to what I have to say. Your boyfriend owes me a lot of money. He took a lot of drugs and time from me. He hasn't made any effort to contact me and since every time I come around here to collect, you happen to be here, you might actually be reliable enough to pay off the debt." The longer he talks the tighter his grip gets and I start to fight him at the end of his rant and he loosens his hold just enough to let me breathe. He doesn't wait long before he tightens again and instead of talking, he pushes his tongue inside my mouth when I try and turn my head away from him he pulls my body away from the wall and slams it hard, back into it. My breath is pushed from my lungs and my head bounces slightly off the mirror. I hear it crack behind my head. "You respect me!" he barks before he lets me go and I drop to the floor. He presses the button to get us moving and I grab my throat in a protective motion.

"Why—" I start.

"Not now baby girl. We will be in public soon. Stand up. You're not an animal." He doesn't look at me when he talks, instead, he just watches the door and restarts the elevator.

When the elevator finally opens Boss leads me out through the lobby and quickly two large men appear to walk behind us. One I recognize as Ace, the other just another man to fear. The stranger walks in front of us and opens the main door before scurrying around us again to hold open the back door to the huge, black Escalade parked at the curb. Boss slides in and reaches his hand out to me. When I refuse to grab it, Ace leans into my back slightly to push me forward. I know that one way or another I will end up in the car, but I don't have to go easily. I stand my ground and fold my arms across my chest like a toddler does at the beginning of a tantrum, Boss leans across the seat, "You're kidding right?" When I don't respond, he sits up and snaps his fingers.

Fear makes my body quiver and I glance around me, trying to find a way out. Ace steps back a bit and I bolt. I don't hear them chasing me, but I also know not to look back. Just as I reach the end of the block Ace jumps out of the Escalade that somehow, quickly yet quietly, sits at the intersection in front of me. I turn to run the way I came from, and see Boss standing only a few feet from me. He takes a step towards me and I stumble back into the chest of Ace, who wraps his arms around me and clamps a hand over my mouth. He lifts me and throws me in the backseat of the vehicle. Boss and Ace sit on either side of me, I assume to prevent me from jumping out of the moving vehicle.

The inside of the Escalade is huge, the back seats are set farther back than in normal cars, so far back that you could easily fit another row of seats between us and the front seats. If all the high tech and luxurious gadgets weren't in the way that is.

"She is quite pretty Boss. Are you sure you won't share?" the stranger says from the front seat.

"Quiet Johan," Ace replies. He leans forward and presses a small red button on the back of the seat and it raises a privacy screen between the front and back. He then reaches into the small cooler and throws some ice in a small glass before pouring scotch into it and handing it to Boss. He sits back and throws an arm over the seat behind me and starts to run his fingers through my hair. I try and pull away, but I am stopped when he pulls my head back with my hair. He puts his lips to my ear and whispers, "Come on little lady, I'm the nice guy."

Boss relaxes next to me and watches Ace run his hands in my hair and across my shoulders, he never goes further than that, which surprises and relieves me. Boss reaches towards me and grabs my thigh tight in his hand before reaching into his pocket and pulling out a small vial filled with white powder. My naivety takes over and I watch him in fascination as he pours a small amount onto his hand and inhales it through his nose. He hands the vial to Ace who pours some out onto the top of my now exposed shoulder and copies the same inhaling technique Boss used, unlike Boss who wiped the residue on a napkin, Ace licks what is left off of my skin and then up my neck to nibble on my ear lightly.

Boss takes the vial back from Ace and offers it to me. I shake my head no, but he didn't like that answer, so he pours some into his palm, sticks his finger in his mouth to wet it and rolls in the white powder then shoves his finger into my mouth. I am tempted for a moment to bite down as hard as I can, but I think otherwise when the horrid taste registers in my mouth. I try not to gag outright, and only half succeed. "The first time is always the worst, but if you snort it like a good girl, you wouldn't have to taste it." Just as Boss finishes his sentence we come to a stop and Johan opens the door for us to get out.

Chapter Eleven

SAMANTHA

Boss pulls me from the car, and we stand in front of a night club, but not just any club. Xenon. This is one of the nicest clubs in all of Seattle. I glance down at my clothes and scoff at myself and Boss glares down at me. "Don't worry, we have other clothes," he says, then pulls me along beside him into the club. We walk back to the VIP area, but we keep going and we enter what I assume people could call the VIP of the VIP. The lights are low, strippers dance on the tables with no clothes on, alcohol is poured at tables and the familiar smell of sex fills the air. Boss leaves me standing in the room and walks to one of the working girls, He talks to her and she looks over at me with pity in her eyes. She walks up to me, grabs my hand, and leads me to the exclusive bathroom.

"I'm sorry you're here babe," she says, locking the door behind us. "Coco is my dancing name, but you can call me Ira."

"Samantha."

She looks me up and down. "A southern belle?" I go to respond but she interrupts me, "Your accent isn't strong, but I have friends down south and can hear you masking it." Ira pulls a duffle bag from inside the small closet and starts to rifle through. She pulls out a small dress and hands it to me, soon followed by a pair of very tall white high heels. I stand there, unable and unwilling to move. "Look, little belle, I know you are scared, but if you don't change, Boss will have my ass too." I shove down the little bit of emotions that had been coming back from the depths of my soul, and turn on autopilot. I strip off all my clothes except my panties and slide the tight, very revealing, white dress over my body. The front of the dress barely covers my nipples, the hem hits maybe two inches below my pelvic area, the back missing, as in non-existent. I laugh to myself because the amount of material used in this dress wouldn't be enough to cover a small child. I know that it's the point, but still. I look at the heels and huff out a breath. "They aren't as hard as they seem, I promise," Ira says. She bends down and helps me put them on, I was always considered a tall woman at five foot eight but now I am easily almost six feet tall. Ira looks me up and down again and ruffles my hair and cleans tearstained makeup off of my face before she leads me back out to Boss's table.

When I approach, I can see Boss's eyes rack over my body and when I go to sit down across from him, he grabs my wrist and pulls me into his lap. He wraps an arm around my waist and whispers in my ear, "You look much better. I hope you like your seat." I inwardly flinch but abstain from doing so in a way he can see.

All night long, women come and try to sneak conversations with Boss and Ace. Men come and go much quicker, they just want a deal and then they leave. At about one a.m., a fat man comes up to our table with a briefcase in hand. Boss must recognize him or do regular deals with him because he looks over at Ace and swiftly moves me from his lap to Ace's. "Don't fucking move," he grunts quietly in my ear before he walks away, fat man in tow.

Ace grabs a hold of my hips tightly and I am surprised by his hold, considering the amount of alcohol and drugs he has consumed, I would have thought he would be out like a light by now. He sits up and grabs a hold of my face, forcing me to focus on him. "This is not the life for someone like you. I'm sorry he picked you," he stumbles across his words but the sincerity in his face still gets through. Ace presses his lips to mine softly and only for a second before he leans back into his chair again, still holding onto my hips.

After a while, Ace starts to move underneath me a bit more, shuffling his feet a bit, flexing his hands against my sides and hips, his breathing sharpens for just a moment before he shoots up, nearly dropping me on the floor in his haste. With me halfway hanging on his side he glares down and forces me upright. He holds me by the upper arm and looks at me for just a moment before tossing me on the seat behind him.

I'm not sure how long I sit here, alone. I think about walking out, and when I look around the room everyone else is gone too. My body won't let me. I know what Boss gave me earlier wasn't much, but it defiantly is getting out of my system, I'm starting to crash, and hard. I kick off Ira's heels and try and get comfortable in the chair I was left in. At some point, I fall asleep because I wake up for only a moment when Ace picks me up and carries me out of the club and back to the car. I know it was him from his distant aftershave. Boss smells like cigars and scotch while Ace smells like expensive champagne and he has the distinct smell of a man, musky in all the right ways that draw you in and make you want to stick around awhile..

Chapter Twelve

MAXWELL

THE AMOUNT OF HATRED AND DISAPPOINTMENT I FEEL for myself is astronomical, I can only imagine how my family feels, how Sammy feels.

"Last time I was here I told myself it would be the last time. Don't all addicts say that though?" I hate talking at these meetings, but Lincoln swears they are for the best. Even though he isn't in recovery he is the closest thing I have found to a sponsor. He keeps reminding me that he isn't one and to find a real one, but I just don't trust people that well.

"Well, Max, lots of times people fail at recovery because they stop trying to be sober. It's a daily battle you have to fight," the lead counselor answers. I shake my head, not because I think he is wrong, but because I know he is right. I got cocky with myself and now I am back here again.

I wish I could say that I am surprised Sammy hasn't

written to me, but a part of me hopes she hasn't given up yet; even as selfish as that sounds.

"Max, you have a phone call. They said it's important," one of the nurses hollers into the meeting room. Our counselor excuses me and I take the phone from the nurse.

"Hello?" I say into the phone.

"Max. Where is Samantha?" Emma asks.

I shake the cobwebs from my head, "Emma, I have been here for two weeks, why are you asking me?"

"I haven't seen or heard from her since you left. She isn't answering her phone. Ally hasn't seen her. Her parents haven't seen her," she rushes on.

"Emma take a deep breath for me okay?" I hear her take a couple of breaths before I continue. "I haven't talked to her since I left either, I gave her a key to my place—"

"Yeah I know, I went there, and your little note and key was inside the door, I think she slid it inside," she interrupts. "Look. Don't come home yet but if you hear from her please have her call me. I'm worried."

"Yeah. Of course. Same to you. Give my brother my love." Emma hangs up before she replies. I try not to take it personally, but it still stings a little.

Just as I go to walk back into the meeting room a familiar Escalade pulls up out front. I step to the office desk, "If those men ask for me, I am not here."

"THEY LEFT THIS LETTER FOR YOU," THE RECEPTIONIST says as she hands me an envelope, "I didn't say that you were here, but they also didn't ask."

I toss the envelope into my back pocket, afraid to open it. I walk to my counselor's office and knock on his door, "Hey Nathan, do you have a minute?" Nathan waves me in and I tell him everything that happened on the phone with Emma and then I reach for the letter. "The guys I use to run with dropped this off and I don't think I should open it alone," I confess.

Nathan leans back in his rolling chair for a brief moment before leaning his arms on the desk between us. "I think that you are probably right. I am honestly surprised that the front desk gave it to you before it went through searches." He gestures for me to go ahead and open it. My hands shake as I try and rip the letter open. When I finally get it open, I pull a folded up note out, when I open the note a small baggy filled with a brown like power drops to my lap.

I stare down at it.

I swear it stares back.

I want to scream.

I want to run.

I want to get high.

"Now Max, you have two options," Nathan starts. He gets up and comes to the front of the desk to lean against it. "We can go get rid of it together, or you can leave right now and use." I look up at him, desperately wanting him to take it away from me or to tell me that it's okay to use just one last time. Nathan is a no-bullshit kind of guy and I respect that, but sometimes I just wish he would make it easier for me. "I will make you fight for your recovery, Maxwell. This isn't easy I know." I don't answer him. "What are you thinking right now?"

"I think I want to go get high," I grind out.

He crosses his arms over his chest, "But you haven't left my office yet."

He says that as a statement, not a question but I answer anyway. "I also want to know what the note says but I can't stop staring at it." Nathan doesn't say anything, he doesn't move, hell he barely breathes. I reach for the bag, stop for a moment before I touch it and I quickly grab it and slam it on Nathan's desk. "I'm not using today."

"Say it again."

"I'm not using today," I say a little louder.

"All right then, lets read the note."

"For ol' time's sake. Boss, Ace, and the southern belle." I read it aloud so Nathan can help me through this.

"I thought Samantha wasn't into the drug scene Max?" Nathan asks.

"She isn't."

Chapter Thirteen

SAMANTHA

I WALK THROUGH THE CLUB AGAIN TONIGHT AND I START to recognize some of the faces. Ira is here almost every night, Boss and Ace escort me everywhere I go, and a couple of the bartenders and I have spent some very personal time together. Boss hates letting me out of his sight, but whenever a man is on my arm while we are in the club, he doesn't seem to mind as much. Maybe it's just because he can monitor me and make sure I don't mess things up for him.

One of the frequent bartenders, Nix, walks up to Boss's table and reaches for my hand. I look over to Boss to gauge his reaction, and before I can stand to follow Nix, Boss starts, "Are you going to start paying for my woman?"

"Payin'?" Nix asks.

Boss leans forward to put his elbows on his knees and sighs heavily before continuing, "Yeah Nix. Paying. She isn't just a club whore, she is mine." I throw myself back in the seat. Boss acts like he owns me but, in all reality, when we aren't here, I stir up so much shit for him I'm surprised he hasn't kicked me to the curb or killed me yet.

Nix reaches into his back pocket and pulls out a couple of baggies and tosses them on the table. When he looks back at Boss, his eyebrow is arched in a "look at me tough guy" way. Boss sits back in his chair again and pats my thigh in a go-ahead motion. Nix watches, and then reaches for my hand again and this time I don't hesitate to grab a hold and let him lead me to the private office in the way back.

Nix pushes me up against the door once it is closed and he starts to kiss along my jaw. I push him back enough so I can get around him. I reach into the front of my dress and pull out the same baggies Nix had just given to Boss and I shake them between us.

"You sneaky bitch." Nix double-checks the lock on the door and walks to me.

"I'm not important enough to pay that much attention to," I remark. He grabs the bags from my fingertips and starts to pour them out onto the desk in perfectly straight lines. He takes a couple of lines and gestures to me to follow suit. Something about coke gets me all hot and bothered. I absolutely hate using the drug, but if it lets me escape for just a few moments, hell yeah, I will do it. Boss and Ace have made my life a literal living hell. By now I should be back home in Georgia, living my best life. Instead, I am doing coke off a dirty desk in the back of a club with a bartender who is about to fuck my brains out.

I kick off the heels I'm wearing and lean over the desk to take my line. Ira taught me how to separate Belle, as they call me here, and Samantha. I am not this person.

Nix wastes no time ripping his clothes off and once I am standing upright, he takes a long stride so he can reach me, he turns me and unzips my dress just to push it to the floor. Without missing a beat, he pushes my head forward so my ass is pointing out at him. He grabs a handful of my hair and slams himself into me. I groan, not in pleasure, more in disgust with myself. He starts to rock himself in and out of me, as the drugs hit me harder, I become numb. I can't feel his body slamming into mine, I don't feel my hair being ripped from my scalp, I don't feel the pain in my knees when he finishes and drops me to the floor like a piece of trash. He doesn't say anything to me as he dresses and leaves me alone in the room.

I sit on the floor of the office. Silently crying. Boss hates to see my tears. I hate for him to see them, it makes me weak. I wipe away the tears and quickly redress myself. I look over at the desk and see a line left. I know my limits with this drug, but every night I push them a little further. I inhale the remaining line. I stand up as straight as I can, and make myself half presentable before walking back to the main room, hating myself even more than I did ten minutes ago.

Boss made me this way.

Maxwell made me this way.

Chapter Fourteen

SAMANTHA

"IT'S BEEN THREE WEEKS. I THINK IT'S FINE," BOSS answers. I look at him questioningly. After holding me hostage for three weeks, he is finally letting me call my mom.

"Really?" I clarify.

"Yes, Belle. Call her now." Boss hands me his cell phone and just holding the phone in my hands threatens to make me cry. I dial her number as fast as I can.

"Hello, this is Annie," my mother answers.

I hesitate for a moment as it almost doesn't feel real, "Mom?"

"Oh. Samantha honey! Where are you? Are you Okay?"

Ace thumps the back of my head and I look up to see Boss throwing daggers with his eyes. "Mom. I don't have much time. Please call Emma. Tell her it's all Maxwell's fault."

"Honey, you're scaring me. Are you Okay?"

"Just call her, please." Ace grabs the phone from my hands and hangs it up.

Boss kicks the chair out from underneath me and wrinkles his face when I groan as I hit the floor. "I told you that you aren't getting away."

Chapter Fifteen

MAXWELL

AFTER SIXTY-SEVEN DAYS IN REHAB, I FINALLY FEEL ready to leave and get my life back together. When Ace and Boss dropped off the letter all those weeks ago, it definitely set me back, but I refused to let it break me. Jackson and Emma only called one other time, and that was to ask when to pick me up today. As I walk out of the front door Jackson is standing in front of the passenger side door. The door keeps hitting him in the back of his legs, but he stands like a statue, I can hear Emma yelling at him to move and I smile, just seeing my family and hearing their voices in person changes my entire attitude. All of Emma's yelling gets baby Christopher riled up and daddy bear cannot help but go to his child. Once he does, Emma flies from the door. At first, I think that she is just happy that I am coming home, but once I see her face I know that I am way, way wrong.

Emma stomps up to me, points a finger in my face and

starts to yell, "What the fuck are you thinking? Have you lost your fucking mind? You better fix this Maxwell or so help me!" Tears start to run down her face, and she punches my chest a few times, not hard enough to cause bruises, but enough to get my attention.

"Emma!" Jackson calls as he comes around the car. "Get back in the car please." She doesn't miss a beat when she turns to get in the backseat with her son. Jackson walks to me and throws an arm around my shoulders before walking me to the car. He doesn't say anything as we load up and I am still at a loss as to why Emma was screaming at me.

"Is someone going to tell me what just happened?" I ask hesitantly. I look at Emma behind me and she stares fire into my soul until I look away and look back at my brother. Again, he doesn't talk but his body language says enough. He sits straight and rigid in the seat, both hands gripping the steering wheel so tight that his knuckles are turning white, and his eyes stay focused on only the road ahead of him. It's a long drive back to Seattle, and doing so in silence will be rough.

Emma starts to complain about being hungry. "We are only an hour from the house, can you wait?" Jackson asks.

"I wouldn't mind eating too," I chime. Both of them throw visual daggers at me. Jackson reluctantly pulls over at a gas station. After Emma disappears inside with Christopher, I look over to my brother, but before I can ask what is going on, he raises his hand to silence me and barks, "Just wait 'till we get home."

WE PULL UP THEIR HOUSE AND I SEE THAT EVERYONE'S cars are there; Charles, Uncle J, Allison, Lincoln, and an unfamiliar little Honda. Knowing that Jackson and Emma are pissed at me for something, I know what this get together is not a good ol' welcome home dinner party. I follow Emma into the house taking a couple of deep breaths before crossing the threshold. I look around the living room and see everyone stop in their tracks to stare at me, subconsciously I think that I have something on my face or that I must look like a stranger to them, the expression on their faces says that something is wrong and they that they are mad that I killed their puppy, when though I didn't. Jackson takes my bag and sets it to the side of the room but nonchalantly blocks the hallway as if I will run away from what they have to say.

A tall, thin, older blonde woman walks up to me, and before I can introduce myself, she slaps me across my cheek. I instinctively grab my face as the burning sensation that heated my face starts to subside. "Annie," a large, manly, man yells as he comes around the corner from the kitchen. She whips her head around to him and I see it. She gives him the look that Samantha has given me so many times.

"Where is Sammy?" I question. The large man catches Annie's hand before she can strike me again, but I flinch anyway. I scold myself for letting rehab make me a pussy but quickly reset my brain to the here and now. "Seriously. What is going on?"

"Look, mister, I know you don't know me—Dean, by the way—I'm little Sam's father and we are here to take her home." Dean's thick southern accent makes some of his words harder to understand but the point is made. Everyone makes their way to a seat in the living room and I sit across from Dean.

"Sir, I thought she would be back home by now. I haven't seen or heard from her since I left town."

Dean shakes his head in disappointment and Jackson starts talking, "Maxwell, it's been almost five weeks since any of us has talked to her, before that no one saw her after you left. She called her mom from a blocked number and we couldn't trace it either." I look to Annie, hoping that she will tell me more about what happened but also hoping she doesn't slap me again.

"Go ahead, Annie," Emma soothes.

"I barely even recognized her voice. She sounded so distant, so broken." Annie's words are broken up by a few quiet sobs before she continues, "All she said was to tell Emma that it is all Maxwell's fault. I had no idea who you were, I thought maybe someone was pulling a prank on us but before the phone call was dropped, I could hear her scream." She grabs onto my hands tightly. "I had to hear her scream, she was so scared. And it's all your fault." She spits the last part.

"I don't understand, why didn't you guys call me? You waited for five weeks?" I ask the whole room.

"I heard a man in the background, he was bossing her around. He sounded so rough and mean." Annie shakes her head at the idea of her daughter being around someone like that. I sit back in my seat and let out a deep belly breath, I rub my head as I try and process everything they just told me.

Emma stands behind Annie and rests her hands on her shoulders in a loving way, "The boys will figure it out. Let's get some fresh air." Annie and Emma kiss their husbands and walk to the back door, Ally falls into step behind them.

"You're going to find my daughter, and you will bring her home to me," Dean says before standing to follow the women outside. Linc, Charles, and Jackson move closer and stare at me like I have the answers. I throw my hands into the air, "What am I supposed to do, I've been gone. I tried calling her cell phone so many times while I was in rehab that I figured she just blocked me when the calls stopped going through."

"Samantha said it was all your fault. What happened when you left?" Jackson asks. I think back to that day and recount everything I can remember. It isn't much and I don't think that it helps much because everyone seems even more confused then they did before.

"Emma said that she went to my apartment and found the key that I gave Sammy. Did you guys check the cameras in the hallway."

Charles walks behind me and smacks my head, "You twat. Of course, we did. The footage is missing for that entire afternoon, we can see Samantha arrive but then it cuts out after she slides the key under the door."

I grab the back of my head in a protective motion. "Well I had to ask."

"Who would do something like this?" Linc asks. "I just don't understand who would want to hurt Samantha, she is so nice, and the timing? It's too perfect."

"She had already quit her job, most of her stuff was already shipped home, she was seeing all those guys, and wasn't going home every night." I look at Linc and question how he knows that last part, but I don't have time to worry about that now.

"Who wants to hurt you?" Jackson questions.

"Lots of people," I answer solemnly.

Chapter Sixteen

SAMANTHA

PAIN ZIPS THROUGH MY BODY.

After the call with my mom is ended abruptly, Boss reaches over and grabs me by the hair and pulls me face to face with him.

"Are you trying to scare her? Do you want to go home, little Belle?" Before I can even answer his questions, his sinister laugh fills my ears. He drops my hair and kicks at my legs, making me fall over again. He stands over me and stares at me in an evil, sadist way. "Maybe you need to be taught a lesson, yeah?" it's not a question.

Ace picks me up and places me back on my feet in front of Boss, but he doesn't let go of me. Boss circles us, like a lion, stalking his prey. His fingers dip into the cleavage of my shirt but he drops his hands and stands back away from us only long enough to look me up and down. He steps forward again and grabs my shirt in both hands and rips it in two. My once tightly confined breasts bounce-free, and Ace looks over my shoulder and hums his approval. While Boss contemplates his next move, Ace changes his grip from my arms to my breast and he starts to massage them in his hands. I want to fight him but at this point, my body is so tired and beaten that I almost don't care anymore. Out of all the men that I have messed around with since Boss took me, neither he nor Ace has tried anything, other than the stolen kisses here and there. My body starts to react to Ace's hands and my body instinctively softens against him. A shallow growl comes from his chest and I can feel his cock getting harder through his jeans that rests against my backside. Boss grabs under my chin hard, and jerks my eyes to meet his, with a little shrug to his shoulders "You're mine. But I'll share with Ace this time." I want to be a smart ass and ask him about him sharing me with all the other men at the club but I stop in my tracks when he grabs the tray off of the table with the now so familiar white powder. He cut me off yesterday morning, said that I was going to kill myself if I kept using as much as I was, which makes me think that my death isn't his goal. If only he knew that it isn't my goal to die but instead, I just don't want to feel anything.

He runs the tray under my nose too quickly for me to get anything off of it, but my body still reacts and quickly. Being this close to my next high makes me start to sweat, and my mouth goes dry. My anxiety skyrockets knowing that within inches is my next fix. In the back of my head I know that this, this right here, is addiction. How I let it get this far, I can't say. I lick my lips and Boss laughs again. "Want some?" he teases. My body nods yes but my brain says no. I don't have a chance to verbalize my words before Ace wipes his finger on the tray and puts it underneath my nose, I inhale as fast as I can, afraid that he will tease me and take it away again. Even though it wasn't much on his finger it was enough to get my head on straighter, and I almost instantly feel better.

Boss puts the tray back on the table and does a quick line himself before he stands in front of me again. He raises his hand and caresses my cheek, his hand slides around my head and he pulls my face to his. His mouth covers mine completely and all I can taste is alcohol and another woman. I pull my head away at the idea of another woman's juices being on the tongue that is wrestling with mine. I did it so subtly that Ace just turns my head and takes my mouth. He pulls back almost immediately and pushes Boss away from us.

"You tell her that you will share her with me but come here tasting of another woman. You're a pig." Boss steps away from us farther and looks at Ace like he just performed the biggest sin of all time.

"Do you have anything else to say, *Dante*," Boss chides.

"Oh, really *Ray*, you want to pull out the name card. Grow up." They continue to argue and Ace, or Dante, whatever his name is, finally lets go of me, and I run to the room they have given me. Even if it has no windows or doors at least it is my own little space.

I hear loud crashes and as the shouting between them continues on, I eventually fall asleep to the sound of skin clashing against skin.

I awake later in the night, Ace crawling into bed with me. "What are you..." I start to ask.

"Shh. I just want to apologize for earlier and let you know," he lowers his voice to barely a whisper, "somehow, someway, I'll get you out of here." I sit up in bed at his words and he wraps his arms around me and lays us back into the bed. He kisses my temple and soon falls asleep.

I lay awake thinking about what he said. I ask myself if he truly means it, or if it's like the time at the club when I first got here all over again, sweet and then sour.

Chapter Seventeen

SAMANTHA

OVER THE LAST COUPLE OF WEEKS SINCE THAT NIGHT, Ace and I have started to spend more time together. He hasn't brought up what he said that night and neither have I, but our relationship is stronger. He no longer tries to kiss or touch me in the ways he did before. I know he wants to, because he sleeps next to me every night and I can feel his hardness rub on my legs and backside as we cuddle.

We lay in bed together again tonight; I roll over to face him and he opens his eyes and even in the dark room their blue depths are easy to find. "Did you mean it?" I ask.

He brushes a few of my blonde locks out of my face and doesn't ask for clarification. "Yeah I meant it."

"Thank you," I whisper and kiss his cheek before snuggling in closer to him. Even if I can get out of here, I know that I will never see Ace again and a small piece of my heart breaks for that.

I AM LOSING MY MIND.

My days only consist of drugs, alcohol, and sex.

I am losing my mind.

I want to go home.

Tears stream down my face as I sit in the shower and my shoulders start to shake from my sobs.

I hear the door creak open and I hold my breath.

"Belle?" Ace whispers through the shower curtain. I open it and let him see that it's me and his shoulders relax some. He puts his fingers to his lips in a shushing motion and strips off his clothes. My eyes widen as he undresses. He has scars all over his chest and I cannot help myself from wanting to run my fingers over them and hear all the stories. When he strips off his pants and boxers, I have to almost physically stop my jaw from dropping. I knew that he was well endowed from feeling him in bed, but he is much bigger than I thought. I snap my thoughts back to the moment but before I can ask him what he is doing he steps into the shower behind me. "I think we can talk here as long as we stay quiet." I nod my head in understanding. I look up and down his body again and I giggle a little bit under my breath. "What?" he laughs.

I gesture down and say, "I'm not sure if talking is what your member wants to do."

"My member? Who the hell calls it that?" he jokes, and I shrug my shoulders in response. "I can't help it if my 'member' likes what it is seeing."

I cock an eyebrow at him. "Did you just compliment me?" Ace shrugs one shoulder.

"I want to get you out of here. And soon," he whispers. Instant tears run down my cheeks, but they go unseen as they mix with the stream of the shower. "We just have to come up with a plan."

"Boss won't let me leave. I don't know what we can do."

"Your boyfriend is home. I've been keeping tabs. Maybe I can reach out to him and see what he can do."

"I don't..."

"Max is home," he clarifies. My head snaps to him.

"No. He is the reason I am here," I say through my teeth and Ace just shakes his head.

"If only you knew," he murmurs and I cock my head to the side a bit in question. "Ever since Boss saw you that first time, he was going to take you. He wouldn't stop talking about you. It was a coincidence that Max also owes him."

"I still would have never been at his place if he wasn't part of my life."

"You just want to blame him so you can walk away from him." It isn't a question, but I still feel like I need to answer him.

"Stop acting like you know what is going on. You're wrong." He throws his hands up in a surrendering motion.

"We have to do something. I will not watch you die."

I interrupt him this time, "I'm not going to die."

"Oh okay," he says sarcastically. "I see you, Samantha, I know what is going on in that head." I notice that it's the first time he has ever used my real name and being the sensitive person, I am another stream of tears start to fall. Ace wraps his arms around my neck, and I rest my head on his chest. The shower water makes our skin slick against each other and Ace audibly groans. "I have to go take care of this." He points to his groan after he releases me, and he hops from the shower. I laugh a bit and finish washing off my body before I get out too.

Chapter Eighteen

MAXWELL

"ALL RIGHT. LET'S MAKE A LIST THEN," JACKSON OFFERS.

I get up and walk to my bag and grab my cell phone off the top of it.

"What are you doing?" Linc asks. "We have to do this now."

"I know you guys are worried, I am too. But you guys waited five fucking weeks, so I think taking ten minutes to call my sponsor real quick isn't going to make much of a difference." I see all the guys share a glance, but they get it. I step out on the front porch and call Ace. Something inside my heart tells me that she is with them. Lying to the guys isn't the most ideal situation but this is personal.

"Hello," Ace whispers.

"Is she with you?" I ask.

"I'm trying to help her." My face heats in anger knowing that I found her this quickly and knowing where she is but not being able to do anything at the moment. I have always liked Ace, seems like a genuinely good guy just a little broken.

"What does he want?"

He lets out a long sigh. "Honestly, her. Something about her gets to him. He is obsessed."

"Is she okay?" I hate to ask but I have to know.

"You know I will never lie to you." I nod my head even though I know he cannot see me. "No. She needs to get out of here."

"Has he hurt her." My anger starts to rise, I don't know what else I should have expected for him to say. My little Sammy is locked up with one of the biggest and most ruthless drug dealers in all of Seattle. He doesn't answer my question which is answer enough. "I'm going to kill him."

"Don't go making rash decisions. Me and her are making a plan all right?" He ends the call then and I walk back inside.

"Are you ready now?" Uncle J asks.

I look to Jackson. "I need you to call Jeremy."

"Wow, why do we need a lawyer?" Uncle J asks.

I walk to the back door and wave to the girls to come back inside. Once everyone is in the living room I start. "She was right. This is my fault." I take a couple of deep breathes and look down at the floor before I begin again. "I know where she is."

"Where?" Multiple voices chimes.

"Let's go get her then." Jackson and Emma stand.

"It's not that easy. Raymundo Sands has her."

Linc rubs his hands down his face, and asks "Your dealer?" Everyone looks between me and Linc then, clearly with a lot of questions.

"Yeah. Boss is the guy I would buy all my drugs from. He is mad at me. I may or may not owe him a lot."

"A lot of what? Money? Drugs?" Uncle J asks.

I finally take my seat again, but I keep talking, "One thing that Boss hates the most is for people to waste his time. I think that he is pissed that I don't want to be one of his little lackeys."

"Should we call and ask him how much money he wants?" Allison asks from behind Linc.

"I don't think he wants money," I answer.

"You still haven't said why you need a lawyer," Uncle J adds.

I sit back in my seat and think about the best way to say it, so I decide to blurt it out instead. "I'm going to kill him."

"I'm going to kill him."

"Samantha, you're not going to kill Boss"

"Ace. I can't stay here anymore. I am so tired," I complain.

"I know." He gets interrupted by his cell phone ringing and when he looks down he recognizes the number, he jumps up and walks away from me, just out of earshot. I can see him through the window and something about his posture and the hard set of his jaw says he is having a difficult conversation. He turns his body and our eyes meet and I see his heartbreak. When he hangs up I watch him bow his head for a moment and he rubs the stress from his forehead before he comes back to me.

"Who was that?" I ask as soon as he enters the room.

He looks around the room and once he makes sure that no one else is paying attention he whispers, "Max."

I shoot up, "I fucking told you not to call him."

"He called me!" he shouts back. A couple of the other

people in the club turn to look at us but quickly move on. "He knows you're here. I didn't have to tell him that."

"I don't want him involved."

"I know." And Ace does know that. Ever since our chat in the shower earlier today, I think that he gets me more than I let on. He pays attention to me. "I told him that we have it under control."

"Even though we have no idea what we are going to do?" I ask.

"I have an idea. You might not like it though."

Chapter Twenty

MAXWELL

"Jeremy is on his way," Jackson says after he hangs up his phone. I nod my head.

"If you guys don't mind, I need a minute," I admit. No one tries to stop me as I walk back to the spare bedroom.

I told Jackson and Emma that I could stay at my apartment, but they insisted that I stay with them for a little while once I came home. Now I almost wonder if that was so they could have me help find Samantha.

I lay back on the bed and I cannot get her out of my head. I always think about my little Sammy, but now my thoughts are filled with concern and dread for her and our future. I know Boss, I know how hardcore he is. The more I think about him even touching her makes my skin crawl and I want to kill him even more.

There is something about rage. It is addictive in it's own screwed up ways. Rage gives me the sense of euphoria that drugs use to and right now I am craving it.

I try to bring myself to think back on the good times

with Samantha, when she was safe. Remembering those are hard though, as all my memories are clouded by an alcohol and drug haze.

I remember the first time I met Samantha Williams.

I was extremely intoxicated, and I showed up at my brother's dinner party super late. I remember her peeking her head around Jackson's shoulder to get a look at me. When her brown eyes met my steel blue ones, I knew. I knew right then and there she was the one, and I didn't even know her name.

She was someone I wanted to be a better man for. All she knew, was I was some drunk asshole that crashed his brother's party.

A knock on the bedroom door pulls me from my foggy thoughts and Ally slowly opens the door.

"We have never met eye to eye, you and I," she starts.

"I made a lot of mistakes. Hurt everyone. A lot," I confess.

Ally sits next to me on the bed. "I know that you never meant to hurt her. But Max, you need to stay away from her." She's got my attention and I jerk my head to face her. "Lincoln and I have talked about you, her, and everything that is happening. We think that it would be best if you two just weren't...you know, you two."

"Oh, so now you speak for my best friend. Since when do you give a shit about what Samantha and I do?" She goes to interrupt me, but I stop her, "You don't care about me in the slightest. And if you truly cared about Samantha, you wouldn't have let her fight her feelings and thoughts alone."

"What are you talking about?" Her anger and frustration start to become apparent.

"You think your friendship is that great? Really? If it is so great, why does Samantha call me crying at three a.m. about how much she misses home or how lonely she feels here in Seattle?" Ally doesn't answer, instead, she looks down at her hands as they twist in her lap. I'm not trying to be a complete asshole to Ally, because she has been a friend to Samantha for many years, but something changed. "Do you know what she has gone through? Do you know what she fears?"

"Do you?" Ally shouts.

I get up and start to pace the small room and think about how to answer her without spilling all of Samantha's secrets. "Yeah. Actually, I do. I listen to her Ally. That's all she wants. If you want me to leave her alone...someone has to listen to her. I mean, all your focus goes to her. She is not okay."

"Do you know something that I don't?" she questions, and I just shrug my shoulders before answering.

"No one calls an alcoholic and tells them all their secrets in hopes that they will remember."

NOW THAT JEREMY IS HERE, I CAN FINALLY GET MY PLAN together, we fill him in on all the details that we have and he looks to me, Jackson must have told him that I have some crazy ideas on how to get her home.

"I'm going to kill him."

"No, you're not," he replies.

"How much time will I do if I do?" I ask.

He lets out a deep breath and rubs his eyebrow before he answers, "Could be ten years, could be life. At this point, it might even be considered pre-meditated. We can come up with another solution."

"Like what? He is a ruthless, piece of shit, drug dealer. You think he is okay with just handing her over?"

"Well, we got Emma, back didn't we?"

"That was different. And her ex did end up dying," I correct.

"A week later, in the hospital. No proof that we did that," Jackson chimes in.

"Have you asked him what he wants?" Jeremy asks.

"Are you serious?" I ask in all seriousness.

"Well? You called me here, I have to try and be a little bit logical."

"No. I haven't called him."

Jeremy shrugs his shoulders. "Does it hurt to try?"

"Maybe! If he knows that I want her back he could hurt, her more!" I shout.

"Didn't Ace tell you that Boss is obsessed with Samantha? He won't hurt her any more than he already has," Jackson tries to reason.

"What if I just want to hurt the motherfucker for taking my girl?"

Jackson puts a hand on my shoulder; "I've been there, and it sucks big time." Emma comes over and grabs my hand in hers and tries her hardest to soothe me through her touch. It's the thought that counts but it isn't working right now.

"Just call him," Emma whispers.

Reluctantly, I reach for my phone. Once I reach his contact information my hands start to shake, not in fear but in the uncontrollable cravings I have knowing I am about to talk to someone who could get me high within the next five minutes. I press the call button and quickly put him on speakerphone but silently tell everyone else to stay quiet.

"I knew it wouldn't take you long to come crawling back to me little Maxi pad," Boss says through the phone. I cringe at the nickname and I don't respond right away. "What are you looking for coke? Tar? Ladies?"

"Only one thing I am after Ray."

"Whoa. Pulling out the name card are we, Maxi?"

"How much?" I ask.

"You know my rates."

I have to physically hold myself together, so I don't freak out on him over the phone, "I already told you, that is not what I want."

"Then what do you want Max?" Boss asks.

"I want my girl. How much?"

"There isn't enough money in the world to give you back my little Belle," Boss mocks.

"How much to get her back and for you disappear from my life, forever." Boss doesn't answer which just infuriates me more. "One million." I offer and he laughs. "Five million?" Boss thinks about it for a moment before he huffs out a breath.

"It isn't that easy, Maxi. See you wasted my time, that is worth a lot more to me than anything else in the world, more than your money, your life, your girl." He ends the call before I can argue with him.

I turn to my friends and family and all I want to do is scream. I let Boss see that I am weak when it comes to Samantha, he knows I will give up everything to get her back. "I told you that money isn't enough for him." I get up and storm out of the living room, again. This entire situation is fucked up and I'm afraid I've made it worse.

Chapter Twenty-One

SAMANTHA

BOSS LIKES TO TORTURE ME IN WAYS THAT DON'T MAKE sense. Sure, use and abuse my body but don't fuck with my head. As he hangs up the phone with Max he looks down at me in front of him and laughs.

"Don't you find it ironic that your little boy toy called to bring you home and here you are, on your knees with my cock in your mouth. You disgust me," he says as he pushes me away from him and stuffs himself back in his pants. How I disgust him when he forces me to do these things baffles me. I don't know how he lives with himself.

Ace sits on the couch behind me as I continue to sit on the floor. Again, this man sees the tears at the edges of my eyes, I hate showing my weakness to any of the people around me, but somehow, Ace is always around when the last brick of my wall falls.

"When I come to bed tonight, be ready," Ace spits at me. I know he is trying to sound like an asshole in front of the other guys, but this is not like him to say things out in the open about him even going near my room. I blink at his sternness and as Ace walks away, following all the other men, he turns back to me and winks.

I finally stand from the floor and Ira catches me as I stumble on my now numb and weak legs. "That boy. He would kill for you."

"What are you talking about?" I ask.

"Ace. That man would do anything you ask. Boss has been through many women and I have never seen him look at one of them the way he looks at you."

"I don't know what you mean."

Ira shakes her head at me in disbelief and after making sure I am stable on my feet she walks back to the stage. I know what she means though. I have been nothing but honest with Ace though this all and he knows that I care for him, just not in the way he cares for me. It scares me to think that he would do something so serious as to kill someone for me, but then again, I know that if Max is out there, worrying about me, he too wants to kill someone.

ACE SITS ON THE EDGE OF MY BED WHEN I AM FINALLY able to pull away from Boss.

"I have a plan. But you aren't gonna like it," Ace whispers. I sit down next to him and he wraps an arm around my shoulders. "If you listen to me, this can end tonight." I jerk my head to him with pleading eyes I beg him to tell me what I need to do.

"First, go take a shower and get all cleaned up, and I'll walk you through it."

Chapter Twenty-Two

SAMANTHA

"Do you think he will let me do it?" I whisper to Ace.

"Yeah, he is an idiot. Do you think you can do this though?" I nod my head yes because I don't have any other options, no matter how much I hate the idea.

I knock on the door to Boss's room and a woman answers but once Boss sees that it is me he shoos her away. "Come in my little Belle." I walk to him and sit on his lap, something I have never willingly done before.

"What brings you to my quarters this evening?" It amuses me that he tries to be all proper, and by evening does he mean two in the morning? I bend my head down and kiss along his neck and over to his mouth.

"I know you were displeased with me earlier today and

I want to make it up to you." I push away my robe and stand in front of him.

He slides in his seat a bit and reaches a hand into his sweatpants to grip himself. "That is one thing that could make any man happy. Belle, your nudity is something to die for." I swallow my pride and take my hands and rub them up my sides and massage my breasts. I start to sway slightly to the nonexistent music, and I let one of my hands creep down towards my pussy. Boss grabs my hand to stop me and he throws his hand around my neck in his oh, so familiar, dominating way. He backs me up to the door I entered through and slams me against it hard. "Now that you have entered my domain, you will play by my rules," he growls in my ear as if I haven't already been playing this twisted game his way.

Boss pushes his clothed body against my naked one and grinds himself there for the briefest of moments. He looks me in my eyes and for half a second and I see he is a human behind the scary monster that he presents himself as. My thought is quickly destroyed when he lets go of my throat and drops me to the floor. "I need to get high before I can fuck you." Given that he is a disgusting man I shouldn't have expected much more from him, but those words still sting a bit. Boss leans over his table and brings a glass pipe like item back with him. He kneels down in front of me, and as he makes eye contact, he lights the brownish powder and before he exhales, he forces his mouth onto mine, making me inhale what he releases. The burn is worse than the burn of the cocaine, so I automatically know that this is something else. He takes another hit and repeats his previous action. I can tell he knows that I want to know what he just gave me, but I also know that he won't tell me. A new kind of numbness spreads across my chest and arms, the pain in my throat from his hands disappears and all the bruises on my body seem to not hurt as much, I start to feel very tired and I have a hard time keeping my eyes open. I feel Boss's hand under my chin as he lifts my face to meet his. "You really are a lightweight." He reaches into the pocket of his sweats and in the familiar motion he dumps white powder on his hand and puts in under my nose. I inhale deeply and the high is different, the mix is something I could see people liking, a lot.

When he goes to pull his hand away, I run my tongue along the area that the powder just sat, and I take one of his fingers and suck on it in a teasing way. He grabs me by my hair as he stands up, pulling me up with him. He walks me to the edge of his bed and in seconds he too is nude. He pushes me hard in the middle of my chest, forcing me back onto the bed. He straddles himself over my legs cradling them between his. Both of his hands wrap around my throat, only one hand is needed given his size, but he still uses both, and he presses harder than before and watches my face as I start to gasp for air. My mouth opens to scream with what air I have, but I don't make a noise. Instead, he spits into my mouth and releases his hands. Before I have a chance to catch my breath, he kisses me hard and deep, forcing his tongue into my mouth and licking along the line of my teeth.

I fight my willpower and I let him continue, one of his hands reaches my chest and he roughly handles my breasts. I slide a hand in between us to stroke his hard length that rests on my stomach. No words are exchanged, before he maneuvers his legs between mine and he raises my legs to wrap around his waist. The only warning I get that he is about to enter me is that he breaks the kiss to look down at himself, he lines his cock up with my opening and he thrusts hard into me. I let out a gasp in pain as he roughly pounds in and out of me. He throws a hand over my mouth and once I realize the amount of noise I am making, I feel bad that Ace is sitting outside the door waiting for my signal.

Boss pulls out of me and roughly flips me onto my stomach. He grabs my hips and thrusts into me again, this time I was more prepared, and the pain wasn't as bad. He continues to pound into me when he reaches under the pillow and pulls out a needle full of brown liquid. I start to pull away, thinking that he is about to inject me with something.

"Don't worry babe, it's all mine," Boss grunts out.

He grabs a hold of my hair and pulls back on it like the reins to a horse. I moan in pain and he mistakenly thinks its pleasure and he starts to pound harder, pushing me forward over and over. In one swift movement he flips us over, so I am on top of him and he pulls himself free to turn me to face him. He thrusts up into me again. "Ride me. Hard," he barks out. I follow his commands, but he still places his hands on my hips and pushes me down harder and grinds my pelvis against his. No matter the pain I feel, I keep going. He reaches to the nightstand and grabs his tie and wraps it around his arm as a tourniquet, I am naive, but I know what he about to do. He finds a vein quickly, but he doesn't inject. He looks at me watching him and pausing my grinding. "Push it in"

"What?" I ask breathlessly.

"Push the plunger in once the needle is inside." I look at him in pure shock. Ace was right, Boss does trust me to an extent, which scares me more than anything. Boss places his hands on my hips and starts to rock me against him lightly. Once I get into a rhythm he likes, he returns to putting the needle in his arm. Once he gets it inside, he nods to it and I place my trembling hand on it. I stop grinding on him and slowly push the plunger in. Once the needle is empty, he tosses it under the bed, but he doesn't untie his arm. "Ride me as hard as you can, when I release the tie I want to come all over your insides." I have to remind myself that this is all part of the plan, but it still is overwhelming. He extends his non-tied arm and slaps my face, hard. I do as he says. I throw myself against him hard and I can feel him getting harder and starting to pulse inside me within seconds. Boss reaches across and releases the tight tourniquet; he throws his head back and comes so hard I can feel his semen hitting my internal walls. After he starts to come down from his ejaculation high, he pushes me off of him and sits up in bed.

"You will stay the night in here," he demands, "I always share my bed with a woman after sex."

Not long after, Boss starts to snore. I watch him sleep for a few moments. I study his features. It looks like once upon a time, Raymundo was a very attractive man, nice bone structure, and despite the drugs, he has a good body, and his dark hair lays across a once handsome face. Part of me feels bad for what is about to happen, but then I remember everything he did to me and I can only imagine what he did to others.

I creep from the bed and quietly knock on the door three times, signaling Ace that Boss is finally asleep.

As Ace opens the door, I put my finger to my lips in a shushing motion. We both sneak through the room. Ace walks to the small table that Boss was sitting at earlier and he starts messing with all the drugs on it. He motions for me to go back to the bed and as softly as I can, I crawl in next to Boss. Ace is soon at the side of the bed with another needle completely full of the same brown liquid. Boss rolls over onto his back, perfect. I crawl on top of him and kiss across his cheek, over to his mouth. He moans underneath me, and I feel his hardness against my thigh. "Oh, little Belle, you just couldn't get enough of me." I kiss him harder and I take his tie and cover his eyes before he has a chance to open them. "You like to play too?"

Ace grabs another tie off the floor and hands it to me, I wrap it tightly around his arm like he did before, and I lean down to his ear and Ace inserts the needle.

"Never again will you hurt me, or anyone else. I wish I could say that I'm sorry."

As I finish, Ace is already done injecting Boss. I quickly untie his arm and uncover his eyes. He looks around frantically, he makes eye contact with Ace and flips him off before he looks at me, wrapping his hands around my throat again, and pushing harder than before. Almost instantly, I'm gasping for air and Ace pulls me from Boss's loosening grips.

The amount of drugs Ace gave him is probably six times the amount he took earlier. He starts to fall asleep, his pulse weakened against my throat before I was pulled away. I watch as he struggles to get from the bed, and he falls forward. His breathing becomes slower and slower.

Flashbacks of Max, unconscious on his bathroom floor, appear in my mind's eye. Ace pushes me away from him and places himself between me and Boss. I watch the life drain from Raymundo Sands, a moment I will never forget.

Chapter Twenty-Three

SAMANTHA

"WE NEED TO GET OUT OF HERE. NOW," ACE BLURTS. I rush past him and run to what was my room and quickly dress in the clothes I was taken in. It only takes a moment to realize that the clothes are much too big now. The drugs and lack of food have taken a bigger toll on me than I thought. I toss them aside and grab shorts and one of Ace's T-shirts from the floor. Ace appears in the doorway then. "Are you ready?"

"I don't want anything from this place, so yeah." I follow him downstairs and out the back door. Ace throws his leg over the motorcycle sitting next to the shrubs and he gestures for me to get on behind him.

"Hold on to me tightly." I clench my thighs against him and wrap my arms around his waist. He doesn't ask me for directions, he already knows where I want to go.

What seems like forever later we pull up in front of Emma and Jackson's home. I jump off the bike and fall to my knees in front of the house. Full, large tears fall down my face. Ace shuts the bike off and helps me stand. "Let me help you inside, please?"

"Ace?"

"Yes, honey?"

"What if...after they see me...they don't want me?" I say between my sobs.

"Don't you ever say that!" He barks. "They are your family. Family doesn't give up on each other." He pulls me into a tight hug and kisses my forehead.

"Thank you. For everything."

"I'm sorry I couldn't get you out sooner." He walks with me up the front steps and as I hesitate to hit the doorbell he reaches and hits it twice and rapidly pounds on the door. Lights flick on in the hallway and I step back from the door. I see the silhouette of a large man coming to the door.

Jackson swings the door open and starts, "What the hell do you want? Do you know what time it—" As soon as he sees me, he reaches past Ace and wraps me in a hug. "Samantha," he whispers. "Please sir, come inside," he says as he pulls me inside too.

"Sit down, please. I'm going to go get Emma. Okay?" I nod my head, and Jackson turns and practically jogs to their room. I hear Emma shout and she comes flying down the hallway. She throws herself at me and wraps her small frame around me.

"Oh my god, Samantha. We have been so worried about you. Your parents are here. Max is here. Everyone is here." I flinch hearing that my family is here too knowing that I worried everyone so much when I had no control.

Jackson walks back toward us but before he gets to the

end of the hall he turns and goes back to the spare bedroom. He knocks on the door and I hear his voice.

"What the hell, Jackson?" Maxwell asks.

"You need to come out here, now!" Jacksons says.

"Why? What's wrong?" Maxwell says, panic in his voice. I see him walk down the hallway towards me, but he is still trying to get Jackson to tell him what is wrong, so he doesn't notice me. I stand, afraid of what is to come. Jackson turns to face him and then he walks past him to the other side of the house where the other spare rooms are, I assume to wake my parents.

Max finally focuses on us. He looks through me for a half a second before he realizes who I am.

"Sammy?"

"Hey, Max," I say shyly. He walks up to me and practically pushes Emma out of his way. He wraps his arms around me tightly and whispers in my ear, "I'm so fucking sorry, Samantha." He barely has time to get the words out before my mother and father round the corner and swoop in to take control of the situation. Everyone starts asking me a million questions and I can't answer any of them. I cannot look into anyone's eyes and tell them the things they want to hear. Max backs off, noticing me shutting down to all of it. Emma notices too and interrupts.

"Let me help you get cleaned up and we can all talk in the morning, it's very late," Emma offers. I nod my head in agreement, and my parents both kiss my head before returning to bed. And I follow Emma to her room.

EMMA HOLDS ONTO ME AGAIN WHEN WE REACH THE bedroom. "I'm so glad you are home. We all have been so worried about you." She steps back and walks to her dresser and pulls out a pair of sweatpants and a tank top and hands them to me. "Do you want to shower?"

I just nod my head. She leads me to her bathroom and starts the water for me. Unashamed after everything I have been through, I start to strip off my clothes. I forget that Emma is not used to seeing me like this, but I push on. I can feel she her staring at all my bruises and cuts, I feel her judging me as she sees my bones showing from the lack of nutrients. I feel like she is burning holes in my soul from her unbreaking gaze and not knowing what to do or say. The scrutinizing look in her eyes makes me feel like I made a mistake coming here.

"Thanks," I say as I step under the spray of water. I watch her walk from the room and I slide to the floor of the shower and let my tears run full force.

I am scared of the future.

I am scared of rejection.

I am scared because I know I will come off of the drugs for the first time soon.

I am scared because I don't have to be scared anymore.

I am safe.

Chapter Twenty-Four

MAXWELL

"I KNOW I REALLY DON'T WANT TO KNOW, BUT HOW DID you get her out?" I ask Ace.

"Just know that Boss will never be a problem for any of us again. You have a strong woman in there, but she is scared, and she is alone. Watch out for her," Ace pleads.

For the first time I can think of, I hug a man that is not my family. "Thank you."

"I care about her. I will check in on her."

"Yeah of course. The moment she says it's too much you will stop."

"If."

"If?" I ask.

"If she asks me to stop. She may never admit this, but she cares for me too. We went through a lot together in the past few weeks. It wasn't easy for either of us." He pats my shoulder and walks out the front door, saluting the family as he leaves.

Emma comes from her bedroom and walks up to all of

us. "She is in the shower. I don't know what she needs but we all need to be here for her."

"I'll crash on the couch so she can sleep with you, it might make her feel better being next to someone she is familiar with," Jackson offers, and Emma quickly agrees.

"I don't want to overwhelm her, so I'll be in my room and I'll talk to her tomorrow. Will you let her know?" I ask. Emma agrees and follows me back down the hallway before going back in her room.

Chapter Twenty-Five

SAMANTHA

EMMA SLEEPS BESIDE ME, BUT I STILL CAN'T CLOSE MY eyes. I fear that this is all a dream and that I will wake up next to Boss and have to live another day with him.

Even though I know I will regret it later, I crawl from the bed and walk to the room Max is in. I knock softly and crack the door open; the lights are off, and I can hear Max snoring. I'm tempted to turn around, but I cannot make myself do it.

I sneak onto the bed next to him and I rock his shoulder a little bit, "Max?" I whisper. "Max?" I repeat.

"Huh?" he questions.

"Max. I need to talk to you," I say. He finally stirs awake enough to process actual thoughts.

"Sammy? What's wrong? Are you Okay?"

"I need to talk to you," I repeat. Max sits up and rubs the sleep from his eyes and he leans over and turns his bedside lamp on.

"What's up Sammy?"

"Can I tell you some things and you not tell everyone else?" I ask.

"Since when have you not told me everything?"

I shoot him a quick glare and continue.

"Well, Boss. He umm. Well, he made me use. I'm scared." Max shoots up straighter and grabs my shoulders lightly.

"He made you use. What a fucking piece of shit! What were you using? Do you know?" he rapidly fires questions at me.

"Mostly cocaine, but tonight he made me inhale some brownish powder."

"Heroin," he says matter of fact. I lay back against the duvet and start to cry all over again. "You will be fine. You'll be a little sick in the morning from that, but the coke will be harder. You will be anxious, mad, emotional, and tired."

"Great, everything I already am," I say.

Max chuckles under his breath, "Yeah, but a lot worse. I'm sorry to laugh, I just know how you feel."

"Can I lay in here for a while?" I ask.

"Of course." He slinks down in bed again and throws the covers down so I can crawl in. I cuddle close to him, which I know he wasn't expecting.

I fall asleep with him holding me tightly against his front.

I wake before Max and wiggle my way free to make my way to Emma and Jackson's kitchen. I start to brew a pot of coffee as I watch the sun rise higher and higher in the sky. My stomach starts to turn, and I can feel myself starting to sweat harder the longer I have gone without any drugs. I push through the wave of uneasiness and just as the last few drops of coffee enter the pot my father walks into the kitchen.

"Heya, sweetie. How ya' feelin'?" My father's southern accent is thicker in the mornings and it makes a smile spread across my face and my heart.

"I'll be okay Daddy." I look up at him and all I want is to be a little girl again and have my daddy save the day. "I want to go home."

He walks to me and wraps his large arms around me and rocks me side to side a little bit, "Okay, I'll have momma book us a flight for this mornin'."

One thing I can always count on with my parents is that if you say you need something or want something with your whole heart, they will make it happen.

An hour later, they have all their bags ready and we are in a taxi heading to the airport. I beg them not to stay long enough to say goodbye to everyone in person. I am already struggling with my emotions, and I have a lot of physical repairs that are needed. Saying goodbye will just hurt that much more. I left a sealed letter in the baby's room for Emma, telling her all the mushy things I don't have the lady balls to say in person.

I need to start over, and in my heart of hearts, I know that going back to Georgia is the right move for me. Boarding the flight is the easy part, it is staying in my seat and not turning around and running back to my friends that is hard.

Chapter Twenty-Six

MAXWELL

WITH MY EYES STILL CLOSED A REACH MY HAND OUT AND feel the cold sheets next to me. My eyes shoot open and I quickly sit up in bed and look around the room for Samantha. I jump from the bed and think to myself that it was all a dream, her coming home. I hear Emma and Jackson in the kitchen talking as I walk down the hallway.

"Where is she?" I ask as I pour a cup of the coffee that is already brewed, believing more now that it was real. Emma slides an envelope across the counter to me and I recognize Sammy's handwriting almost instantly.

My dearest friend,

It hurts too much for me to say goodbye in person and I'm sorry this is how I am doing it.

I went through a lot in the past few weeks and I need to go back home. Momma and Daddy are with me, and I will be ok.

*Once I get a new phone, I will call you. Hug Jackson
for me, and thank him for everything that he has done, give
baby Christopher all the auntie love you can for me.*

Let Ally know I love her.

Tell Maxwell that I'm sorry.

Talk soon,

Love ya'll bunches.

Sam

I toss the letter on the counter and look at my little brother, "She is sorry? What the fuck for?" I scratch my head and pick the letter back up and read it again, and again, and again. "Isn't it weird that she signed it as Sam, not Samantha? Did she really just up and leave like that?

Emma places her hand over mine and rubs small consoling figures across my skin. "She might not ever admit it Max, but she is so in love with you it is disgusting. I'm not sure what she is apologizing for, maybe just for leaving without saying goodbye. As for her signing as Sam...it threw me off for a moment too. Back in the day, she used to go by Sam, then things changed and maybe she is just trying to find herself again." She shrugs her shoulders at the end because she is as unsure as the rest of us.

"I need a meeting," I say before I walk back to my room to get ready. As I pass by them again, I see the letter in the same place I left it and I snatch it up, fold it nice and small, and place it inside my wallet before I walk out the door.

Chapter Twenty-Seven

SAMANTHA

THE PLANE LANDING IN ATLANTA'S AIRPORT JERKS ME awake and I feel my whole body starting to hurt again. Max prepared me for this, but it still hurts. I stretch my body as much as the seats will allow once the seatbelt light turns off and everyone around starts to stand and my mother leans towards me.

"Once we get in the cab you can nap some more honey."

The cab ride back home is a long one, but as soon as I see the sign reading, "Welcome to Lovejoy Georgia" I feel like I can finally take a deep breath. I'm far away from all the things that happened to me and I feel my chest rise with newfound hope.

FOR SIX LONG DAYS, ALL I HAVE DONE IS EAT, SLEEP, CRY, and shower. The detox from the drugs is no joke. I thought about Max a lot throughout the harder moments, knowing that I judged him for using over and over again, when now that I am in his position, I understand the craving just to feel better. Now I feel almost normal and I need to get my life together. Make a plan for what I want, and what I need. I pull a piece of paper from the junk drawer in my parent's kitchen and make a list of all the things I need to do. Top of my list though, get a real cup of coffee.

I sit outside the small coffee shop, enjoying the fresh air, and thinking. Before everything, I took advantage of the little moments, that will not be me anymore. Taking time to be with myself and thinking is a luxury that I didn't have when I was with Boss.

I asked my parents this morning if I could stay with them a little longer than we originally planned and they didn't seem too keen on me leaving the nest again. In time though, I will be okay enough to leave. The feeling of homesickness that I felt while in Seattle diminished the moment we landed in Georgia. This place makes me happy and I will never go back.

I look down at my to-do list and mentally check off the coffee. I toss the paper into my small purse and walk down the block to go get a new cell phone and computer, since both disappeared when Boss took me.

It doesn't take the techs long to get me set up with all new gear and as I head back to my mother's car that I parked next to the coffee shop, I look across the street and see a for sale sign in the window of a cute corner building. Large, broken picture windows frame the shop, beaten flower boxes sit rotting on the sidewalk, and the front door seems to be hardly hanging on to its hinges. I walk back into the coffee shop and ask the teenager behind the counter if she knows anything about it. She just shrugs her shoulders and moves on to the next customer.

As I walk back outside, an old man stops me. "Excuse me, ma'am. Were you just asking about the building across the way?"

"Yes, sir, I was," I answer tentatively.

"Would you sit with me for a moment? I want to tell you about that spot." He gestures over to the building and sits at one of the small tables just outside the doors of the coffee shop. Not having any other plans, I sit with him.

"That was my wife's shop, once upon a time. She sold the most beautiful flowers and she was the nicest, and the best looking florist in all of Georgia. Why are you asking about the shop?"

"Something about it pulls me in." I cannot explain to the old man what my thoughts are because I don't quite understand them myself. He leans forward on the table as if settling in for a long story. "I grew up around here, and for some reason, I am just now noticing the place." I rest my elbow on the table, then my face in my hands, and stare across the street for a moment.

"You have the same look she did," he says.

Looking back at him I ask, "And what look is that?"

He lets out a long breath, "The look when a woman falls in love. They only give that look three times in their lives you know. When they meet the man of their dreams, when they hold their children in their arms, and when they find their passion."

He sits back again and turns to face the building. "Suzanne, my wife. She looked at that building, and she knew right away that it would be hers. You have that same look." I blush at his kind words.

"I'll give her to you," he blurts.

My head jerks back to face him, "What?"

"If you promise to take better care of her than I was able to, and you think about me and Suzanne every once in a while, you can have it." He reaches into his pocket and pulls free an envelope and hands it to me before he stands up and walks away, like a ghost in the wind, he is gone.

I open the envelope and a set of keys drops to the table; a letter stuffed inside.

I never wanted to get rid of this place but if you are holding this letter, then something changed. I am writing this in April of 1974, while sitting at my desk in the back office of my little flower shop.

Some things you need to know about this place.

The floors are original, the stained glass in the back room too.

The faucet in the bathroom drips, no matter how many times the plumber says it's fixed.

The register sticks, so sometimes you have to slap it on the side.

When it rains, leave the door open, the flowers like it that way.

The young man that comes and buys one tulip every day, his name is Thomas, he is my favorite, treat him well.

If my husband is the one who handed this to you, I am gone, and he is soon to follow. I hope that this place gives you as much joy as it did me.

Take care of her,
Suzie

I wipe away the tear that falls after reading the letter. I look over to where the old man had walked away too and I see him as he gets into a cab, he waves goodbye and disappears. I look down at the keys in my hands and I get the feeling that I need to go over there and check it out, to see if this is really happening.

I stand at the front door and slide the key into its lock, turn the old handle, and it opens with ease. I walk into the shop and just like Suzie hoped, I fall in love.

Chapter Twenty-Eight

MAXWELL

"I THINK THAT IT'S A GOOD IDEA," EMMA AGREES FROM across the dinner table.

"Yeah, I do too," Jackson chimes in. "Your office is the same but if you need a change, we can make that happen."

I shake my hand at his offer, "I'm fine with what I had before Jackson. I just need to get back to work."

"Well, if you want to go in tomorrow, we can do our weekly briefing and get you caught up."

I nod my head and look up over my fork as I shove another bite into my mouth. I give him a thumbs up and he and Emma laugh at my actions. I smile around my food and for the first time in a while, I don't have to fake the smile. Being with my family makes life easier, but also harder in some ways. It's been two months since Samantha left, and there hasn't been a single day that I haven't thought about her. I ask Emma every day how she is doing but per Sammy's request she doesn't tell me much. The first week she left I bought probably ten different flights to

Georgia, but I never boarded. I wanted to chase her, hell I still do; but she needs time and space. So do I.

GETTING UP THIS MORNING AND PUTTING ON MY SLACKS and a dress shirt gives me chills, kind of like when we first started this all those years ago. Jackson knocks on my open door and leans against the jam.

"You ready brother?" he asks.

"Yeah. Let me down a cup of coffee first, and we can head out."

I told Jackson last night that I think having him drive me in and then home for the first little while will help me keep myself together, get a new routine that doesn't involve stopping at the clubs or that wherever else.

The ride to the office is peaceful, but because something is wrong with me on a whole new level, I break the silence. "I miss her," I confess.

Jackson looks over at me, "You are just now noticing that?"

"Hell no. I missed her the second she left. I almost followed her you know?" My brother doesn't say anything, instead, he just listens to me talk. "How am I supposed to stay away though? I'm pretty sure she is the love of my life. Jackson..." he looks over at me, "I have never said that about a woman, and it terrifies me."

"I know Emma gave you her new number, have you tried calling her?" he asks.

"She told Emma that it is for emergencies only, she

doesn't want to talk to me." I fold my hand in my lap and look down at them. "What if she never forgives me?"

"Max. She doesn't even blame you. There is nothing to forgive." Jackson turns to me now that we are parked in the garage of the Shaw building. "Look at me." I look up at my little brother and wonder how it ended up that he was taking care of me, not the other way around. "Let's have a guys' night. You, me and Lincoln, no alcohol, no drugs, just some good ol' manly fun and we can talk about all the mushy shit the women think we don't feel." I laugh at his idea, but it sounds exactly like what I need, and I tell him that.

"All right then. Let's get to work."

We both step out of the elevator on the floor where our offices are, I am surprised that things are exactly how they were when I left. The receptionist stands and welcomes both of us and like the true professional she is, she doesn't make a big deal out of me being here. I keep walking to my office when Jackson turns into his, I stand at the door and stare at the minifridge stuffed under the bookshelf, knowing what use to be stored there and afraid that no one removed it.

"Jackson had me clean out your office while you were gone." I jump at Tiffany, my assistant's, voice. "Your fridge is stocked with water and tea. We replaced all the towels in the bathroom, and I cleaned out the stuff in your desk." I look at her, afraid that she will judge me for what she found but all I see in her eyes is compassion. "My brother died from an overdose. No judgment here, and I haven't—and won't—tell anyone."

"Thank you very much, Tiffany. Are you busy this morning?"

She looks down at her planner, "I am free until the weekly briefing, which is in about forty minutes."

"Can you get me caught up, so I don't look like an ass in there?"

She giggles quietly. "Sure."

Like many times before, Tiffany is here to save the day. She has always been here for me in the professional sense, making sure my paperwork was filed, my meetings were scheduled, and ensuring I showed up to those meetings. I never noticed how much I relied on my team to help me function day-to-day.

I make a mental note to myself to thank everything today at the meeting and to get Tiffany a raise.

Chapter Twenty-Nine

SAMANTHA

I HAVE FOUND MY NEW PURPOSE.

After finding the deed and a notarized letter that discusses the transfer of ownership in the broken safe in the office, I called my father's lawyer and got everything legally transferred to me.

Waking up every morning to go and work on the shop has given me a whole new perspective. In Suzanne's letter, she talked about all the issues that happen in this place but each day when I open the door, I see it as a blessing to carry on the stories and love that once was here.

My father has helped me fix up the place a bit. We replaced the broken windows and fixed the front door so it is nice and sturdy and will close completely. My mother cleaned the floors and cleared out all the garbage that has collected since it was closed down. My father has a few of his work friends coming to repaint and check the electrical work today and I have submitted my business plan to the bank for a small loan to get everything I need to open the shop, and should be hearing from them today as well.

I prop the door open with an old brick that I found in the office and let the warm spring breeze blow in. I stand back and admire the room, thinking about how the girls and I somehow missed this building every day when we were kids. I wonder how they would feel about me opening my own store and how they would react to me doing it pretty much alone. For a brief moment, I think about Max too. How he would tell me how messy my business plan is, or how to make sure I price things right, or how to be a business owner in general. I get a pit in my stomach thinking about him. A longing, sad pit, deep inside. I shake myself free of the thoughts and feelings about him. Thank goodness I do, because a work truck pulls up outside and three men jump out and quickly grab primer, brushes, rollers, and all the necessary items to get to work.

The younger-looking of the guys walks up to me and gives me a binder. "Here is a bunch of colors and whatnot for you to pick from, let me know later today and we will get it all taken care of."

"Oh, thanks." I set the binder on the counter and shake his hand as a way of introduction.

"Samantha, right?" I nod my head yes, "Lane."

"Nice to meet you Lane. Thanks for doing all this."

He joins his coworkers and they quickly get to work taping off areas and laying the sheets, so they don't ruin the floors. I grab the binder and retreat to the office and allow them all to work. I power on the new computer that we set up in here and check my emails and a new message from the bank appears.

Samantha Williams,

Your loan has been approved for *Suzie's Spot:
Nursery and Bakery*. **Please come to the office at
your earliest convenience to sign all
documentation.**

I jump up and down in my seat at the good news and
send a text over to my parents letting them know about
it too.

For the first time in a long time, I am able to look at
the future and not cringe at what I don't know will happen.
I'm looking forward to the unknown, I'm starting to
embrace the changes.

Chapter Thirty

SAMANTHA

LANE HAS STUCK AROUND.

Even though the shop officially opens tomorrow, and no construction is needed, he hangs around. Over the past two weeks, he and I have spoken a lot, gotten to know each other, and I would say that we have become almost friends.

"How are ya feelin' about the mornin'?" he asks.

"Good. Super good. Momma is coming down with me to make her famous banana bread and pecan pies. All of the flowers look beautiful."

"What are you doing tonight?"

"Nothing much. Making sure that everything is ready for tomorrow I guess."

"Let me by you a drink." He doesn't ask, he more so tells me. I am reluctant to agree because of everything that happened back in Seattle, but Lane is attractive, he is a gentleman, and most importantly he doesn't know my history. I look at his dark shaggy hair and just now I notice his great physique. My eyes meet his green ones.

"Actually, yeah. I'm down for that. Just let me lock up and we can go," I offer. He gestures his hand out in front of him, shewing me away to complete my work..

We sit at a small table at the bar down the road. Lane quickly orders a beer and a burger, and I do the same. We chat about everything and nothing, he makes me laugh, which is rare these days. I start to let my guard down a bit around him which I know can be dangerous. He reaches his hand across the table and touches my arm. I instinctively pull away and he holds his hand up in an innocent motion.

"Sorry," I say quietly, and I look down at my lap and twist my hands.

"Don't be. We all have things about us." I know he is trying to be nice and understanding, but I'm still on edge and anxious. I close my eyes for a moment and gather myself before I sit back up. I visibly shake my feelings away and as I do, the waitress brings us our order. Lane swallows his beer in a couple of sips and it is quickly replaced with another one. I look at mine for a moment but decide to eat a bit first. When Lane finishes his third beer he points to mine and asks, "Do you want something else?"

"Umm. Do you think they will give me an unopened one? "

"If they don't, I'll kick someone's ass," he says before he gets up and walks to the bar. He is back in no time. A bottle opener in one hand and a sealed beer in the other.

"Thanks."

"No problem Samantha."

I open the beer and take a quick sip before taking a full drink. I watch Lane bite into his burger again and nausea raises in my throat. I take another sip and eat a couple of fries thinking that it is just nerves. Something about this situation seems familiar and when I look back up to see Lane's face, I am surprised that it is him, because for some reason I feel like this should be happening with another man. A man who I have had many meals with. A man that is not here.

"You okay?" Lane asks.

"Yeah, Deja vu, I think." He laughs a little and returns to his meal. I feel myself shutting down from him. I keep trying to eat but every time I do, I feel worse. He makes small talk, but I think he is noticing that I'm not giving this my all anymore.

I take another sip of the beer, and a small tear runs down my cheek. I'm able to wipe it away before Lane notices, but even the taste of the beer makes me miss Max.

I want to call him and tell him all the things that have happened to me since I left. I want to hear his voice. I want to see his face. I want to kiss his lips while we both are sober and let it mean something. But instead, I continue to run. I ran away from him and told him not to follow and here I am wishing he hadn't listened to me, but I refuse to call him first.

"I think I should go home."

Lane doesn't fight me on it. "Okay. Let me walk you back to your car." Part of me thinks that he knows more then he is letting on, or maybe he is just such a gentleman that he doesn't mind that ending things early.

Lane walks me to my car and kisses my cheek before

jogging across the street and hopping into his truck. I sit in the driver seat and lay my head on the steering wheel. I bang my head, harder than I should, against the wheel. I know that I just screwed up my chances with one of the nicest guys I have met in a long time, but my heart isn't ready. I can't stop thinking about Max. I hate him and myself for that.

Chapter Thirty-One

MAXWELL

SIX MONTHS LATER

Eight long, dark, miserable months have gone by since Sammy left my life. She disappeared, and hasn't looked back. Emma still is giving me small updates, just enough to keep me kind of in the loop and to let me know she is ok.

Sobriety is hard when you are alone. It is even harder when the love of your life isn't talking to you and you know that she is struggling too. I cannot blame her for not reaching out, but I also wish she would. I want to give her time and space, but I don't know how much longer I can do this.

Linc and Jackson have been helping me a lot and taking me to meetings, but I think it is time for us to talk it out. So far, they haven't asked me anything about my addictions, nothing about my recovery, they just ask if I'm doing okay or if I need a meeting. Tonight, is guys night, a new tradition that Jackson started, which means that the three of us just get together and bullshit, eat and watch whatever game is on tv.

We all sit in the living room of my apartment and pig out on some pizza, I mentally grab onto my balls and start, "Can we have a talk, guys?"

They both sit up a little straighter and I know they are preparing for the worst. I know that part of them thinks that I am about to tell them that I need to go back to rehab or that I relapsed.

"I just think that it's time to get this out there," I add.

"Are you okay?" Jackson asks.

"Yeah, little brother. I'm ok."

"What's going on?" Linc questions.

I set my food down and think about how to start. "This is going to seem like some girly shit but just go with it. You guys know that I have struggled for a while now, my counselor told me that at some point I needed to talk to my friends and family about everything, but it scares me because I don't want anyone to blame themselves or to get mad at me for having fucked up coping skills."

Jackson leans forward and Linc relaxes into the couch more. "No judgments will ever come from me brother." Linc nods his head in agreement.

"When mom and dad died, I was twenty-two. My life had only barely begun and theirs was ending so suddenly. I didn't know what to do with myself let alone a teenager. Uncle J did everything he could, but I was still falling apart. One night after you went to bed Jackson, I left the house and I had no intention of returning. I was going to leave and never come back, I had a bag packed and loaded into my car and I was just going to disappear. I drove through town and I saw Uncle J's bike at the bar, so I stopped in, something told me that I needed to stop. Sometimes I think back and wonder what would have happened if I hadn't stopped. I like to think things would have been all right but who knows. Anyway, I stopped. When I walked into the bar for the first time something in my brain flipped and I instantly knew that I was going to get drunk enough so I couldn't drive, because then maybe I couldn't leave—that was my thought anyway. Uncle J was talking to some mean looking guys and when I walked up, he acted like he didn't know me. Everything I tried, he brushed me off. Later that night, Uncle J and one of the guys left the bar together and the other one came up to me and asked if I was into partying. Halfcocked and half-drunk I told him, yes and that was the first time I did cocaine."

Jackson lets out a deep breath but doesn't interrupt.

"When I got home later that night, I felt like complete shit. I felt horrible for trying to leave. I felt bad about doing drugs. I felt a lot of emotions that I forgot I had. I never grieved our parent's death. I couldn't. Someone needed to be strong and someone had to take care of things. I made the mistakes I made, and I will always live with them inside of me and I cannot blame anyone for it. In order to hide those emotions, I went back to the bar the next night, then the next, every night until I got kicked out and I had to start buying bottles at the store and bringing them home. It escalated very quickly and all of a sudden, I couldn't control it anymore. I went to rehab for the first time then. I wasn't ready. I didn't know that going in, but I know that now. I relapsed the day I left. A woman was leaving the same day, and she was talking about going and using one more time, just for shits and giggles. She introduced me to heroin, and I watched it kill her. Before I met her, I had never seen it before. I wasn't, and still am not a huge fan of it but clearly, I have used it here and there. I will say it is much cheaper than cocaine. I came back to Seattle and keep on using, constantly being reminded of what it did to her. A couple of years later, Uncle J disappeared, and I realized how much time had gone by. I honestly was only half sober when we started Bradshaw Industries. I'm surprised you let me do anything with this company at the time. I was in and out of detox facilities and rehabs. For years, I gambled with my life. I didn't care what anyone else had to say, I didn't care how much I hurt people, I didn't care what I had to do to get my next fix." I sit back in the chair and throw my hands in the air. "I care now. I feel now. No one tells you that while you're out running the streets you won't care but if you make it through, you will care later on. Our conscious isn't gone when we are using, just quieted."

"I'm proud of you," Jackson says. I look at him in surprise. "I'm serious, it takes a lot to say that all out loud and you're clean and sober right now. That is what matters." Linc nods his head in agreement.

"Things are not okay for me though," I say.

"What do you mean?" Linc asks

"Samantha," Jackson adds.

"Yeah," I answer quietly.

"Emma can call her, and you can talk to her," Jackson offers.

"I have screwed things up so badly with her, but I feel so lost without her in my life. She is my everything and I fucked up by not telling her sooner and by not protecting her." My frustration starts to boil over. "I should have chased her."

"Do it now," Linc says.

"What?"

"Chase her," he clarifies.

"How exactly am I going to do that?"

"It's not like she fell off the face of the earth. We know where she is," Jackson adds.

"Yeah but we also know that she doesn't want to see me. She won't even let Emma tell me what she is doing or anything. How am I supposed to do this exactly?"

"You are miserable, so just figure it out. Would you rather leave it all unknown or would you rather take the chance that she might miss you too?" Linc pulls out his psychoanalytical mind to try and help.

"What was your initial thought when Linc said that you should chase her?" Jackson asks.

"I thought, I still have a bag packed and I can catch the next flight out."

"Then let's do that." Jackson stands and heads towards the door.

"Jackson!" I yell.

"What? I can't and I won't let my brother suffer any longer. So, get the fuck up and let's go." Linc and I both stand and look at each other as if asking if we really are doing this. Jackson claps his hands together to get out attention. "Come on. I need to let Emma know that we are leaving."

"We?" I ask.

"Yeah, why buy a plane ticket when we can just use the company jet, and get there faster."

"What if she doesn't want to see me?" I ask.

"We will handle that if it happens," Jackson says.

"Did Emma tell her we were coming?"

"No, I asked her not to."

I lay back in the seat of the plane and try to close my eyes for the last stretch of our flight.

"Since we are getting there so late, I got us a hotel room so we can come up with a game plan in the morning."

"What if I just move here?" I suggest.

"To Georgia?"

"Sure, why not? I don't have any bad connections here, I can work at our Georgia office, god knows it needs some help. And my girl is here. Even if she hates me, I can still keep an eye on her. Make sure she is safe."

"Is that what you want to do?" Jackson asks.

"I think so. I have been thinking about it for a while. I don't know if I will be able to watch her fall in love with another man and grow old with someone else because I want to be that person for her but maybe someday, we can at least be friends if she doesn't choose me."

"When are you planning to do this?"

"Now. I think. Might as well. I'm already here. I don't

need anything from my apartment in Seattle—it's just all bad memories. I can get a place over here and start over."

"All right then. Seems like you know what you want to do."

"Yeah. I think so." I know my brother doesn't like the idea, but I think it is what I need to be able to start over.

Not long after, we finally land in Atlanta and I think about how Samantha felt when she landed here. Did she have this sudden feeling of peace go over her like I just did? Did she finally feel safe?

Chapter Thirty-Two

SAMANTHA

I HEAR THE BELL AT THE FRONT DOOR CHIME, AND I holler from the kitchen.

"Hang on, I'll be out in just a moment.:" No one answers, but they never really do. I walk out, apron still on, flour all over my arms and face, probably even in my hair. I see the back of two men looking at the photos on the wall. "That one on the end is of the original owner, Suzanne, and her husband, they gave me this building about eight months ago, and I restarted the business that they started." I walk towards them, and continue, "The couple in the middle, those are my parents, next two them is the rest of my family. Jackson, Emma, Allison, Christopher, and..."

"Me."

My head jerks to face the familiar voice, my stomach tightens, and when he takes a step toward me I almost feel like I am dreaming. Max continues to step closer to me in a slow and calm manner and my breathing picks up. Jackson turns around and watches us and gives me a little wave. I lift my arm just enough to wave back but my eyes never leave Max's. He reaches me and using his pointer finger he traces my name tag attached to the apron and reads it off.

"Hey, Sammy." My heart breaks open, instant tears run down my cheeks. Why would he come here, especially no? I was finally healing from all the damage he did to me emotionally. He turns to look at Jackson who no longer is paying attention. Max pulls me into a tight hug and whispers in my ear, "I didn't mean to make you cry, honey."

"Why are you here Max?" I mumble into his chest.

He pulls back enough to look me in the eyes again, "I made a mistake by not chasing you."

"I told you not to. How can you be wrong for doing what I asked? That doesn't make sense."

"I'm wrong for believing that you knew what you needed when obviously it isn't what you wanted, what either of us wanted."

"You don't know what I wanted then, or what I want now," I snap.

"You're right. I don't but I would like to figure it out. If you will let me." I pull myself free from his grip and walk up to Jackson and give him a big brotherly hug.

"We miss you, Samantha," Jackson says.

"I miss you guys too. Things are good here though," I tell them both.

"Can we come by later this afternoon? We have an appointment in about thirty minutes," Maxwell asks. I huff out a breath. "What?"

"I knew you didn't come all this way for me," I say under my breath as I walk back towards the register counter.

Max stops me by grabbing my arm. "Don't get it wrong Sammy. I'm here for you and only you," he grits out.

"He is buying a house here," Jackson intervenes. My eyes snap back to Max and he shoots Jackson a quick glare.

"Why are you buying a house, Max?" I ask.

"I can't be in Seattle anymore. You aren't there. Instead, you are here. So, I will be too."

"What if when you find out what I want it isn't what you thought?" I ask.

"No matter what you tell me. I can't be that far from you. Even if you choose another man, I will always be close by."

"I don't understand why you would do all that."

"This isn't the way I want to explain it all. Please let me take you out?"

"Maxwell." I pull away from him again.

"Just hear me out please?" he pleads.

"Max, whenever you ask me out, its back luck. Every time, something bad happens, or you don't show up, and you break my heart all over again."

"Nothing bad is going to happen and I will be early even tonight. I know it is hard to believe but I really am sober this time." As much as I want to believe him I just can't. Jackson steps around Max.

"He really is clean. Since he went to rehab, he hasn't done anything except read and work."

I look at both of them for a moment. "Seven. This is your last chance, Max. My heart can't handle another blow by you. It's too hard."

"I'll be here," Max says before he walks to the front door.

THE BELL RINGS AGAIN AND I LOOK AT THE CLOCK, SIX forty-five. I walk from the office and fix the tank top that I was changing into. "Sorry, we closed about fifteen minutes ago."

"I have a to-go order," Max jokes.

I smile and a small laugh escapes me. "That was almost kind of funny Max."

"I was going to bring you flowers, but I thought that might be weird," he says as he gestures to the nursery with all the flowers. He pulls his hand from behind his back and hands me a single stick. I laugh at the stick, and he soon follows.

"Now that is great," I say around my chuckles.

"I made it," he announces.

"I see that."

He steps to me and with a gentle touch he points at my chest. "Your heart will never again receive a blow from me."

"I want to believe you, Max, I really do."

"I have a whole evening planned for us, so if you would." He turns to face the door with me and leads me outside. I lock the door and he grasps hold of my hand as we walk down the sidewalk. We walk a few blocks down to the local pizzeria where I sit across from Max, and just stare at him for a little bit. His jet-black hair is a little longer than usual, brushing the tops of his ears when normally it is just barely more than a buzz cut. His steel-blue eyes stare back at me. They are clearer, brighter, more intense. I feel my breath catch and my cheeks heat against his stare.

He breaks the silence. "The first time I asked you out, I was so scared. I was sure you would reject me. When you said yes, I about shit myself and I scrambled to come up with an idea. I hadn't taken a real woman on a date since my twenties, and my first thought was pizza."

"Is this a way to make up for you not showing up that night?"

"Absolutely not. I fucked up many, many times. I can never make up for those. All I can do is move forward." I nod my head in understanding at his words, that is the only reason I gave him another chance. We both need to start over, try again. "You really are beautiful, Sammy."

"Thank you, Max." I blush at his words. I never know how to respond when someone compliments me. I am saved by the waitress coming by and taking our order. The fact that some pizza places do not sell pizza by the slice amazes me, luckily this one does so we don't have to argue over whether or not pineapple goes on pizza, which it does.

I only briefly think about how this same date would have been if I was sitting across from Lane instead of Max. His laughter brings me back to reality.

After eating way too many pieces of pizza and drinking a glass too much of root beer, we walk outside and Max leads me down the mid-town streets. Since it is getting dark outside the streetlights flash on and light the path in front of us. When I think that we are heading back to my shop he turns us the other direction.

"Max, the shop is that way."

"I know. We aren't done yet," he says. He holds my hand again and leads me to the public park and we sit in the swings and just gently go back and forth.

"I'm sorry, Samantha."

I turn my head to him. "I'm sorry too." We both have done so much to each other that the list is too long to say everything we are sorry for. Just knowing that both of us want to move on is a good sign.

"I put you through a lot and I used you when that was never okay."

"I did the same thing. We both did things that we regret but we are here now."

Max stands up and crouches in front of me and my swing. "I love you, Samantha. I never wanted to hurt you," he chokes out the words.

Like the big emotional train wreck, I am I start to cry. "Maxwell. That isn't fair, because I love you too, and neither of us did it on purpose."

Max grabs my hands and lifts me from the seat, he wraps his arms around me, and like a true gentleman he asks, "Can I kiss you?"

I answer by putting my lips against his. He deepens the kiss and places a hand in my hair while the other one sits around my waist. Both my arms snake around his head and neck. I stand on my toes to get better leverage and he pulls back and rests his forehead on mine and lets out a deep breath. "I know that I tried to kiss you a few times while I was drunk, but I don't remember them that clearly, so I'm just going to say that was our first kiss. And holy shit was it the best first kiss I have ever had." I smile into his neck.

"Do you want me to take you back home, it's getting late?" he asks.

"Can we just hang out for a little while longer?" I ask.

"How about I take you back to my room, no funny business. We can just watch a movie and eat snacks all night."

"I think that would be pretty awesome."

Max and I walk into his fancy hotel room, and I bounce on the edge of the bed a little while he hangs up our jackets. He stands in front of me and steps forward and places a leg on each side of one of mine. He bends over and grabs my face in both of his hands and presses his lips against mine again, harder than before. I let us fall onto the bed and Max's tongue dances with mine. He moves a hand underneath my back and lifts my stomach to touch his and he moves me up in the bed a little more. He relaxes onto his other forearm and breaks the kiss. "I promised no funny stuff, but I just had to kiss you again." I push him away playfully and when he falls onto his back, I leap on top of him and straddle his waist. I sit up straight and stare down at this man that has changed my life in ways I would have never imagined. My heart sings for this man and my soul always reaches for him, in all situations.

"When I first moved back, I was asked on a date. I went…He wasn't you though, I had him take me back in the middle of the date because I just couldn't stop thinking about you."

He tries to sit up, but I push him back down. "You are the guy. You are my match." I lean down and brush my lips across his and I hear his breath catch when I do. He grabs onto my hips and keeps me from rocking myself along him.

"Careful now little lady. I won't be able to keep my promise if you aren't careful," he whispers out. I sit back up and put on my pouting face before I roll away from him and pick up the television remote.

"Any preferences?" I ask.

"Pick whatever you want, I'll call room service and get us some goodies."

He didn't seem mad or disappointed that I removed myself from him. Other men, even if it was their idea would still get mad, not Max. I flip through the rentable movies and finally just pick the newest horror flick that is on there. When room service arrives with sparkling cider, fruit, pie, chips, and popcorn, my inner fat girl started to fall for Max all over again.

"You sure you want to watch a scary movie?" he asks as he reclines against the headboard after stuffing himself for the second time tonight. I crawl up next to him and press play on the movie.

All the jump scares and creepy scenes made me grab onto Max tighter and scoot so close that if I was any closer, I would be a part of him. Once the movie is over, he puts on some comedy, and not long after, I am fighting to keep my eyes open. I tuck my head into the crook in his shoulder and before I know it, I fall asleep.

Chapter Thirty-Three

MAXWELL

I WATCH HER SLEEP FOR WAY LONGER THAN A NORMAL person should, but letting myself fall asleep runs the risk of her leaving again. I don't want that to happen, but I also don't want to think that it could happen. Samantha brings the best and the worst out of me. I fear that she will think that the bad outweighs the good. I am subconsciously begging her to let me prove that wrong.

I wake up and start to panic when I don't feel Samantha in my arms. I turn in the bed and she is not there, again. I feel the sheets and they're still warm though. I think to myself, maybe I still have time to stop her, and convince her to give me this chance. I jump from the bed and quickly shove my feet into my shoes and grab my cell and throw it into my pocket before rushing to the door.

I pass the bathroom door and see Samantha leaning in the door jam in one of my T-shirts, which she must have taken from my suitcase and her underwear. "When were you going to tell me that you were still here?"

She giggles and walks to me. She places a hand on my chest and pats gently before reaching up on her toes and lightly kissing me. "At first I didn't know what you were doing. It was kind of funny to see you scramble. I'm not going anywhere, Max." She walks back to the bed and when she lifts a leg to crawl back in the shirt rides up and I can see the small part of her ass cheeks that the underwear doesn't cover. Like a dog going after a bitch in heat I rip off my shirt and kick my shoes haphazardly to the side and I pounce on her. She squeals in excitement and as we collapse together in bed, we both start to laugh and stare at each other.

"I only promised to be good last night," I remind her.

Samantha arches an eyebrow at me, but she knows exactly what I mean. "Good." She leans towards me and plants another solid kiss on my lips.

I raise myself above her and lower my hips onto hers. I press my tongue into her mouth only for a moment before I trace her jawline with small kisses. I nibble down her throat and she throws her head back and arches her back, pushing her chest into mine, a good sign. I push a hand up the shirt she is wearing, and I trace a line up to her breasts, I find that she removed her bra sometime in the night, and I feel myself get harder knowing that she laid next to me almost nude. Her hands travel to my waist and she slides a hand just inside my sweatpants and grabs my cock through my boxers. I groan deeply, and she moans slightly as I tug on a nipple with my teeth through the shirt. She pushes as me and I lift myself up, she pulls the shirt off and tosses it to the side. I stare down at her body and her entire body blushes as I examine her.

"You are so fucking beautiful."

"Not bad yourself old man," she chides.

"Hey, low blow Sammy. And just so you know, thirty-eight is still young enough to keep up with you." I push her back into the mattress, and I kiss along her sternum and to her belly button. I reach her panties and as I pull them downward, I notice a large scar across her hip. I run my tongue along it and ask, "Will you tell me all about this scar honey?"

"I have more scars than people can see Max."

"I like your scars. Physical and otherwise. They make you who you are." I try and break the tension and run my hands over her body again and I somehow manage to get my sweats off without having to stop touching and kissing her. As adults, our make-out session could be seen as juvenile, but I want to go slow with my girl, I want to take care of her and not do something that will make her run. Contrary to popular belief, not all men are pigs who just want to get laid.

She reaches around to my ass and pushes my boxers away and once my cock is free it springs up and rubs between our stomachs. She grinds her body against mine and I rip her panties from her body. I reach a hand down and touch her hot core. I insert one finger and use my thumb to massage her clit. I pump my finger in and out a few times before adding a second one. She moans at the movement and I feel her wall clenching onto my fingers, and I think about how good she will feel around my cock. She reaches for my cock, but instead of trying to put me inside of her, she starts to pump her hand around me; I grunt like some type of beast as she continues pumping with a fierce effort. I have to push her hand away and take a couple of breaths before I come like a boy with his first woman. I pull my fingers from her and I put them into my mouth and suck the juices off them.

I readjust myself, and align my cock with her entrance and watch her face and she looks at me with pure love and admiration in her eyes. Before I enter her, I lean down and kiss her softly, as she starts to get into it, I push myself into her. She gasps at my intrusion and she puts her legs up onto my hips and using her ankles she pulls me into her more. She moans as I start to pump gently, and I watch her facial expressions change as she gets closer to the edge.

I push in a little deeper and a little harder. I groan in her ear as she tightens her inner walls around me. She reaches between us and starts to massage her clit like I was before and something about a woman creating her own release gets me all hot and bothered.

"Oh fuck. Sammy. I'm not going to last long."

"Me either. Harder. Please," she begs.

I lift myself up with my arms and I start to pound into her each thrust harder than the last. Her core has a death grip on me and when she comes, her walls vibrate along my shaft, making me come too. Both of us breathe heavily as we lay there together. I finally pull myself free and clean us both up before I return to the bed and pull Samantha into a close, tight cuddle.

"I love you, so much Sammy."

"I love you Max."

"Later today, can I take you to see the house I went and looked at?" She yawns and shakes her head yes. "Rest first honey, we have lots of time."

WHEN I WAKE UP THIS TIME I DON'T PANIC, I FEEL Samantha's warm skin against mine and I hear her soft snores. I sneak from the bed and quietly call room service for some breakfast even if it is almost lunchtime, I hop into the shower and clean myself quickly in the hopes the Samantha will still be asleep once I'm done. I wrap a towel around my waist and walk into the main room to see her in the same spot I left her. I grab clean clothes from my suitcase and finish dressing when our food arrives. I open the door and shush the serviceman as he wheels in the chart. I tip him well for being so accommodating, but rush him out the door. I check the food and make sure everything looks all right before I wake her. I reach back into my bag and pull out another shirt for her to throw on and I sit on the bed next to her. I lean over and brush her golden blonde hair out of her face, pull the covers down to her shoulder and kiss her forehead. She stirs a bit at the touch but not much.

"Sammy. Breakfast is here." She rolls away from my voice and tucks the blankets around her tighter.

"I see. You are not a morning person." I go back to the food and pour a cup of coffee, toss a couple of sugar cubes into it and take it back with me to the bed.

"Sammy, what if I told you that I have a nice cup of coffee sitting here for you." She turns back towards me and peeks between her hair and the blanket to see the cup I hold in my hand for her. She closes her eyes again. I grab a breakfast cookie from the tray and bring it back to her. Again, I try and bribe her. "I have a cookie and coffee."

This time she only opens one eye, she zeros in on the cookie and snakes a hand from under the covers and snatches it from my hand. I look from my hand back to her a couple of times, surprised at what just occurred. I can barely see her mouth, but I can hear her biting into and chewing the cookie.

"Is it good?" I ask. She nods her head and reaches her hand out for more. I set the coffee on the bedside table and go and grab a few more of the cookies. I hand her one and she quickly pulls it under the covers, she doesn't have time to eat it before she reaches her hand out for the other one, I have.

"Hey, now little lady. Don't be greedy." She laughs from under the covers and starts to sit up. The cookie hangs out of her mouth as she holds the sheet to her chest. Even after everything she has been through, and considering that we just made love this morning she hasn't lost her sense modesty. I reach over her and grab the clean T-shirt I pulled out for her earlier. I hand it to her, she tosses it on like a pro and reaches for the coffee. She takes two full gulps before she relaxes her shoulders and looks over at me.

"Mornin'," Her southern accent is strong when she first wakes up and it makes my heart skip a beat all over again.

"Good morning. How did you sleep?" I ask.

"Great. You?"

"Having you next to me makes everything a hundred times better." I wink at the end and she dips her head and blushes again. I would much rather see her face be red with blushing rather than tears, which I have seen way too much with Samantha. "Don't forget that after I take you to get clean clothes, I want to show you that house."

"Yeah, no problem. Just let me have about three more of these first." She raises the cup to indicate what she is talking about.

I laugh at her actions. "Okay, I won't stop you."

After four cups of coffee and two more breakfast cookies, she is finally ready to go. I take her to her parents' house to change and luckily they both are gone, I don't think that I am ready to face them again after they left the way they did, and I know that they saw Samantha go through a lot those first few weeks home and I also know that they blame me for it.

Samantha walks from her bedroom in tight jeans and a loose-fitting sweater, the weather is starting to turn, and the air is getting cooler. I watch her hips move from side to side as she walks towards me and all I want to do is take her back to the bedroom and take those same clothes off and devour her body again.

"You ready?" she asks.

I have to shake the thoughts from my head, "Yes. Let's get out of here. And away from all the beds." I whisper the last part, but she must have still heard me because she chuckles behind me.

We pull up to the house just outside of Lovejoy and Samantha rushes to get out of the car. I watch her take in the view and I admire it again. It's an old farmhouse, painted a fresh white with a pale-yellow front door. A huge wrap around porch makes the front of the house pop when you drive by. This house is considerably smaller than Emma and Jackson back in Seattle, but I think that it will accommodate our family just fine.

"Can we go inside?" she asks.

"Go ahead."

She leads the way inside, I can almost hear her jaw hit the floor, she looks around the large open room and she looks back at me, "Max, you need to buy this house. It's gorgeous."

"You like it?"

She opens her arms out wide, and says, "Well I wouldn't suggest that you purchase it if I didn't like it."

I blow out the breath I was holding, hoping that she would like it.. I reach into my pocket and pull out a set of keys and hand them to her. She looks at them for a moment before she looks back up at me with a questioning look on her face.

"They accepted my offer on the spot yesterday. I know it is a bit unorthodox, but I want you to move in with me. Here. Help me make this house a home."

She looks around the open space again and then back at me, "do you promise not to just up and leave in the middle of the night? Do you promise to help me move? Do you promise to show up, to everything?"

"I promise, to all of it. I love you, Samantha. I want nothing more to make you happy and keep you safe."

"Then as scary as it seems, I guess I'm moving in with you," she confesses.

Chapter Thirty-Four

SAMANTHA

WHAT IS WRONG WITH ME? WHY WOULD I DO THIS TO myself?

Moving in with Max is probably one of the stupidest moves I could make right now. Does knowing that stop me? Absolutely not. I am still sitting in my bedroom at my parent's house, all my belongings packed into boxes, and the last of my clothes are stuffed into a duffel bag. I wish I could kick my own ass. I am trusting someone who hasn't really ever proven himself to me, my heart and soul jumped in and took over and now my brain is yelling at me. Part of me knows that I am probably making a mistake, but the other part hopes that maybe it will work.

Trying to explain my actions to my parents was much easier than I thought it was going to be. Even though I know both my mother and father held a lot of resentment towards Max in the beginning, my mother at least, listened to me cry about him. She listened to me want him back and then turn around and cuss him out. While they aren't thrilled that I am up and leaving so quickly, they are supportive.

Max stands in my doorframe and leans against it. "You don't have to move in Sammy."

"Do you want me to stay here?" I question, more defensive then I mean for it to be.

He comes and kneels down in front of me as I sit on the edge of the bed. "I want you with me, but I also want you to be happy."

I stand and he rises with me, and I wrap my arms around his waist and just hold myself to him. I know in my heart of hearts that my decision has been made. Fuck the risk.

"Can you carry one of my bags?" I ask.

He pulls himself away from me long enough to plant a hard kiss to my lips. "I'll carry anything you want. Do you want me to put it in your car or my rental?"

"Well, that's actually my mom's car. Emma sold the one I had while in Seattle and I just haven't gone a gotten a new one," I confess.

"I have to get a car too so how about we go tomorrow? Better late than never," he jokes.

He leads the way from my bedroom out to the car parked outside. He tosses my few bags into the trunk so I can go say goodbye to my parents, at least this time when I move, I'm only twenty minutes away instead of across the United States.

We pull up outside the new house and I take a deep breath before I follow Max up the driveaway. Max opens the front door and sets my bags on what would be considered the living room floor.

I start to laugh, and Max looks over at me, question in his eyes. "We don't have any furniture, food, dishes," I say around my laughing.

He starts to laugh too and shrugs his shoulders. "I guess we will camp out tonight and get the basics tomorrow."

One thing I have always loved about Max, he doesn't flaunt his wealth. Even after everything, I know that he is still worth millions and instead of hiring some interior designer to come out and polish up the place he wants to go pick each item out and argue over paint colors and whether or not we get circle or square plates.

WE PICKED UP AN AIR MATTRESS AND A COUPLE THROW blankets at the sports shop in town and we lay in what will be our master bedroom. Max lays on his side, facing me and he traces small shapes on my stomach. Before he says anything, I know what he is going to ask, and I mentally prepare myself to tell him.

"Tell me about your scar?" he asks.

I let out a deep breath and I stare up at the dark ceiling as I start:

"I was a Sophomore in high school, and I got the chance to study abroad in Russia for a few months. I was so excited and the idea of getting away from this small Georgia town, away from the same people, away from my parents, all of it just seemed so amazing." I pause for a moment trying to get my thoughts together. "When I first got there, it was everything I could have imagined. The cities were beautiful, the school was top-notch, it was the people that were the problem.

After being there for a week or two one of my class-mates asked me if I wanted to go to a party with them. I was the popular girl here so going into a new place and being invited to a party seemed like the first step to gaining power; which when I look back it is the most childish thing to say, but it is what I believed then." I mentally shake the cobwebs and start again.

"Anyway, I show up at this house for the party, and there are only a few people milling around. I saw the guy that invited me so I walk up to chat with him, but he gives me the cold shoulder which pissed me off, so I walked outside. One of the guys he was hanging out with followed me out and introduced himself and handed me a beer. I wasn't much of a drinker in high school, but I know that one beer wouldn't get me that drunk.

Not long after, I'm stumbling all over, I can barely func-tion, and the same guy helps me to the couch. Out of nowhere everyone was gone expect him and the guy who invited me. I started to internally panic, but I couldn't get my mouth to work, my lips were stuck together and every time I tried to open them it felt like I was ripping them off. They walked circles around me on the small couch and made jokes about my clothes, hair, eye color, everything. They called me their little baby Sam and ripped my clothes apart. One of the guys had a pocketknife and he cut my bra off." I point to a tiny scar in between my breasts that if the average person wouldn't notice unless you were looking for it.

"He just barely nicked my skin, but I could feel the small trail of blood running down my chest and stomach. While he played with my breasts, his friend tried to remove my pants and when I kicked him for it, he grabbed the knife and stabbed it into my hip. I cried out for help, but everyone was gone. He slid the knife to the side and the blood started to pour out. His friend freaked out and tried to stop the bleeding and they screamed at each other in Russian, so I could barely understand what they were saying. I tried to get up and run out the door, but I fell in the hallway." Max runs his finger across the hip that he originally asked about and follows it towards my back. I sit up then, my back towards him and lift my nightshirt up and I hear him audibly whence when he sees my scars there. "When I hit the ground it made enough noise for them to notice that I wasn't sitting there anymore and one of them took off their belts and pelted my back with the buckle. I only remember the first few blows. I'm not sure if my brain just shut out the pain or if the lack of blood finally caught up to me. I woke up back in the states. My mother sat next to me in the hospital bed and she cried as the doctor explained all my injuries to me." Max traces the scars on my back but doesn't say anything. "No one else knows what happened besides you and my parents. Other men have seen my back, but they didn't care enough to ask."

"What about the girls?" he asks.

I put the shirt back on and shake my head no. "I always had my back away from them if we changed in the same room. I haven't ever once worn anything that showed my back to anyone, and I told everyone not to call me anything but Samantha because they didn't call me by my full name."

Max sits up and sits behind me and puts his legs on either side of me. He rests his chin on my shoulder and swipes my hair to the opposite side. "Thank you for telling me. I know it isn't easy letting it out." I take in a deep breath and lean back into his chest. He wraps his arms around me and holds me for a moment. Max kisses the side of my neck, I know he wasn't trying to be sexual, but after dumping all my trauma out on the floor I feel vulnerable and I want him to make me feel safe. I turn in his arms slightly and brush his cheek with my hand before I pull his face to mine. He deepens the kiss and I finish turning, I push him down towards the mattress and lay on top of him. I kiss down his chest, down to the waistband of his sweats just to use my hands to push them down and I rub my body up against his. He pulls me back up and cradles my face in his hand. Max kisses me again, my hands trace back down between us and I grab a hold of his large hardness and pump him a couple of times to tease him before lowering myself down on him. His fingers find their way into my panties and I rock myself on his hand. Moments later I lift myself from his hand and remove my panties and straddle him again; in one swift movement. I impale myself with his cock and he groans and closes his eyes. I seat myself fully on him and I gasp at the deepness. Neither of us moves as my body adjusts to having him inside me again. Slowly, I start to rock myself back and forth on top of him. He squeezes his eyes shut as his grip on my hips tighten, I place my hands on his chest to get better leverage in my movements and I can feel his chest rumble beneath me.

His eyes pop open and out of nowhere he sits up and holds on the back of my neck and drives himself into me over and over. He pulls my chest to his and nibbles under my ear while he whispers sweet nothings. My clit rubs on his groin and I feel the electricity flow to my toes as I reach my climax. My nails dig into his back and he bits down on my shoulder, harder than I think he meant to. Max gently lowers us back down on the air mattress.

All throughout the night Max and I take turns ravaging each other. The sun starts to rise in the windows, and since we don't have curtains it is very bright as it reflects off of the light-colored carpet.

"Let's take a shower and we can head to town and pick up some stuff," Maxwell offers.

I turn onto my stomach and moan into the pillow, "But it's so damn early."

Max gets off the air mattress and it bounces me onto a cold spot, making my nipples harden to points, and the hair on my arms to stand on end. It makes me hop up quickly, I rush past Max, trying to be the first to try out the shower in our brand-new home.

AFTER WE SPEND ALL DAY SHOPPING AND MOVING THINGS into the house, we can finally say it is starting to feel like a home and not just a house. Max calls and invites my parents over for dinner and we stand in the kitchen chopping vegetables and stirring pasta when they arrive.

"Hey, ya'll," my dad hollers as he enters.

My mother follows close by and carries a small six-pack

of root beer. She tosses them into the fridge and looks over at me and Max. "What? I thought it was funny." She laughs.

"Annie figured that since we can't bring wine or anything the next best thing is pop. When she saw that there, she damn near scared the shit out me when she started laughin' in the middle of the store."

My mother starts to laugh again and once she catches her breath says, "I'm sorry, I know it really isn't funny."

"It kind of is," Max adds, making my mother laugh all over again.

Once dinner is served, we sit at the new dining room table and my parents talk with Max like they are all old friends. Making jokes and taking jabs at each other. My mother tells some embarrassing stories about me but to make me feel better Max shares some of his own, making me fall for him all over again.

My father and Max retire to the living room after dinner to "talk man to man" as my father put it. My mother stays in the kitchen and helps me clean up.

"What are you going to do with this size of a house?" she asks.

I shrug my shoulders before I answer, "Max picked it, I just fell in love with it once he showed it to me."

She comes and stands closer to me and asks, "Do you love him?"

"Yes, momma. I love him a lot. No matter what has happened."

"That's all I needed to hear." She turns and goes back to washing the dishes.

Chapter Thirty-Five

SAMANTHA

I WAKE UP WITH EXTREME PAIN IN MY STOMACH IN THE middle of the night. Max isn't home since he had to drive to Atlanta to work in the office for a couple of days. For the past couple of months, he drives to the office to work for a day or two a week. The longer I sit, the worse I feel, no position is comfortable, and nausea and sweating start to set in. I decide to call my mother, because she is the closest and she drives over to pick me up and take me to the hospital. I lay in bed until she arrives. I hear her foot-steps coming down the hallway and my stress relives some, but the pain doesn't change. She opens the door and rushes to my side.

"Honey, you don't look very good. Come on now." She pulls my blankets back and gasps, I do too when I see that I have blood on my sheets. My panic starts to rise and when I stand up, I feel the blood run down my leg, and I feel slightly light-headed for a moment.

My mother helps me get cleaned up and quickly gets

me in the car and drives to the local emergency room. In the back of my head I think about Emma and how if we were in Seattle, she could've been my nurse. My mother interrupts my thoughts. "You need to call Max, sweetie."

I fumble in my purse for my cell phone and once I find it I dial Max's phone. He doesn't answer right away but when he does, I can tell he was sleeping.

"Hello?"

"Hey, Max."

"Sammy? Are you okay?" His voice raises an octave, indicating his worry. I tell him what is happening, and I try and keep him from losing his shit.

"I'm heading out now. I'll be there soon." He hangs up before can tell him that it isn't necessary, and I don't bother calling him back and trying to convince him to stay. He already made up his mind.

Not long after we pull into the emergency room parking area and we are meet by nurses with a wheelchair helping us inside.

COUNTLESS TESTS ARE DONE.

Maxarrives just at the doctor returns to my room.

"Okay, Miss Williams, and…" the doctor starts.

"Maxwell sir." The doctor looks at me as if to ask if it is okay to talk about things in front of him and I give him the verbal ok.

"I'm Dr. Sierven, I work over in Labor and Delivery, I was asked to consult on your care Miss Williams, we have figured out what is causing the bleeding and pain. After you and I reviewed your medical history I ordered the ultrasound and it looks as though that you had a miscarriage. I'm sorry for the news, but I think that it is important that we do further testing to determine what's going on." He pulls up an image on his tablet that he is carrying and points to a few blobs on the screen. "This here is your left ovary. See the difference between it and your right?" He doesn't give me time to tell him that I don't see a difference. "The left one is considerably smaller and an irregular shape. This..." he points to another spot, "is your fallopian tube. The one over here is misshaped and looks to have a lot of scar tissue surrounding it." He sits down next to me and grabs ahold of my hand. I'm sorry to say, I'm surprised that you even got pregnant naturally, to begin with. I think that if you wanted to have kids in the future it may be extremely difficult, but not impossible. I would love to take you on as a patient if starting a family is what you are looking to do."

I am not shocked at his words when the doctor sewed me up after my run-in with the Russian's he said that fertility may be affected, but that he couldn't say until I was older, and all healed up.

Max's hands tighten around mine and when I look up at him, I see the same devastation on his face that I felt that day. "So, are you saying that we might not have kids?" he asks.

Dr. Sierven turns to him, "I'm not saying that it is impossible. But it will take time and it might not happen, but in all reality, sure it could happen."

I feel some of the tension release from Max after hearing those words.

"Can Max and I have a few moments please?" I ask and Dr. Sierven shakes our hands and says that he will be back in a bit to check on us. Once he is gone my tears start to fall. Max sits on the edge of the bed and pulls me into a hug. "I'm so sorry."

He pulls himself from me and looks me in the face. "For what Sammy?"

"I killed our baby and I might not be able to make more." The tears fall harder and faster.

"Samantha!" he barks at me. "Don't you ever say that again. You did not kill our baby. We can figure this out together. If you want to start seeing the doctor that was just here we can do that. If you want a different one, we will find a new one." He tips my face up to his and I can see the tears gleaming in his eyes; he kisses me sweetly and rests his forehead on mine.

"Do you want to have babies Max?"

"Of course, I do. If we need to get a surrogate or adopt or whatever we need, we can have as many babies as you want. Do you want babies Sammy?"

I nod my head yes and whip away more tears. "Before I didn't. But I want your babies, our babies."

"Then let's tell Mr. Fancy Baby Doctor to get us on his schedule and then we can get you home so I can take care of you."

Chapter Thirty-Six

MAXWELL

TODAY IS THE DAY.

Today I am asking Samantha to be my wife.

I am asking her to spend the rest of her life with me, god be damned all the conventional rules, we have already broken so many of them anyway.

I send Samantha a text to be ready to go to dinner at seven tonight and that I will be home to pick her up then. In the meantime, I have to go talk Dean, her father.

SAMANTHA LOOKS ABSOLUTELY GORGEOUS. SHE'S wearing a tight-fitting dark red sweater dress and black high heels. Her blonde hair sits in soft curls down her back and her makeup is simple and beautiful. She doesn't need any of that crap to be beautiful, but I think that for this occasion it's fitting.

She sits across from me and under the table I fidget

with the ring box that holds my mother's ring. I tried to give it to Jackson when he proposed to Emma, but he refused to take it. So here I am, sweat beading at my brow, and my chest getting shaky from the nerves. I tell myself to grow a pair and I stand up and go to Samantha's side and get down on one knee. She looks over at me and instantly tears threaten to fall.

"Samantha. Sammy. I have put you through literal hell and you still came back. We have seen the best, the worst, and the ugliest parts of each other. Ever since I laid eyes on you that night at my brother's place I knew. I knew I would be here, in this spot. I'm just sorry it took so long to get to this point. I have loved you since that first phone call. I fall in love with you over and over every day. Waking up with you beside me on the air mattress. Making cookies at your shop. Telling stories with your parents. It's all I have ever wanted in my life; I just didn't know it until now. I want to keep doing all of those things with you. I want to build a family with you and create a wonderful future. I know it might be strange to marry an old man like me, but I already talked to your father and if you would, I would really like to get off this floor. So, will you marry me, Samantha?"

She looks at me and I can see the tears running down her cheeks. She opens her mouth to talk but nothing comes out. I start to panic.

Just as I start to think that she is going to say no she finally speaks out. "Yes, Maxwell. I'll marry you."

Chapter Thirty-Seven

SAMANTHA

NINE MONTHS LATER

"Daddy? Am I making the right move?" I ask.

He straightens his bowtie and offers his arm for me to hold on to. "Well honey, you haven't walked in yet, we can still run if you want."

Hearing my father voice my options makes me plant my feet even harder into the ground so much so that I feel my heels digging into the soft carpet of the church floor. I look over at my father and see the big smile on his face.

"Your mother said the same thing to me when we got married you know? She knew that it scared me to get married in front of a bunch of people, but when she said that...I don't know it made me want to stay even more I guess."

The music on the other side of the door starts, the cue for me to walk down the aisle to be given away to Max. The doors swing open and the flower girl, Lincoln's daughter, walks ahead of us tossing small red petals on the floor. My two best friends and bride's maids follow her closely. Leaving only me and my father left. He reassuringly pats my hand, I take a deep breath and I walk.

I look down the aisle and see my family standing around the room and my heart swells a hundred times larger than it should be. My eyes meet with Max's and for the first time, he looks like he might cry. His grin gets larger and larger the closer I get to him. My father places my hand into Max's once we reach him and kisses me on my forehead before going to his seat next to my mother.

Our preacher starts the service. Beautiful ceremonious words are spoken. Lincoln, who stands behind Max, reaches into his pocket and pulls out his cellphone and taps Maxon the shoulder. He tries to ignore him but when he does it again, he starts to turn and Lincoln shoves the phone in front of him. I notice that it is actually Max's phone that was being passed around. Max recognizes the number and apologizes to the entire room, me, and the preacher before answering.

"This is Maxwell."

"Yes ma'am."

"Today ma'am"

"Thank you, we will be there as soon as possible." He clicks off the phone and looks around to everyone. Tears stream down his face, he grabs onto my face and plants a hard kiss, the preacher coughs slightly in annoyance. "Everyone! We are parents!" I look at him in shock, we only applied to adopt a few months ago, after my doctor determined that we would not be able to have children of our own. I playfully slap Max on his shoulder and throw my arms around him.

"Shall we get on with this then?" the preacher suggests, his smile has replaced the scowl he had only moments ago.

Max and I laugh and return to our designated spots so we can finish saying our vows and get to our new child. I have so many questions, desires, and fears running through my brain that I only half remember actually saying the words "I do."

We skip all the after-ceremony events, our friends and family are understanding, and we both hop into the SUV out front with *Just Married* painted in the back window. I toss my bouquet out the window to all the women standing around. We don't stay long enough to see who catches it.

Max speeds down the road and as he hits the highway to Atlanta, I pull our duffle bag from the backseat and quickly change into something more comfortable and much less formal. Max tries to watch me from the side of his eye while still paying attention to the road.

The trip flies by and in no time, we are at the adoption center. Max strips off his suit jacket and tie to look a bit more casual before we walk inside.

We check-in at the front desk and are told to wait in the lobby until our care manager comes to get us.

"Well don't you guys look nice today," the older woman says as she approaches us.

"Nancy. So glad you called us," Max says when we stand to greet her. She motions for us to follow her; we enter her office and we all sit.

"Let's chat a bit about this." She hesitates for a moment

before beginning. "Typically, we don't place children in homes where the parents are not married."

Max interrupts her then, "Funny you say that. When you called, we were in the middle of saying our vows."

Nancy claps her hands together in excitement. "Oh goodie. Congratulations you two." She shuffles around a few papers and tosses them in the trash. "Well, never mind to all those. Mostly legal jargon about custody if something was to occur, but since you are married, it is a little simpler." Nancy hands us a small file, and when we open it we see two little boys, one just barely a toddler and the other an infant. We simultaneously look up at her, question written all over both our faces. "That is Thomas and Ethan. Their parents passed away in a house fire about two months ago. They have been staying with family since but none of them have the means to take on two small children, and they are being put up for adoption. When their file came across my desk, I immediately thought of you guys. Once you meet the boys you will fall in absolute love, and Max, I think that with you having lost your parents too it will be easier for them to open up to you.

We look at each other and we both know we aren't going to turn these kids away. Not today. Not ever.

"When can we meet them?" I ask.

Nancy looks surprised that we are so interested. "Now. They are here." She bounces from her chair and we follow her farther down the hallway to the small playroom.

My eyes contact with the older boy and just like Nancy said, I fall in love. I don't think twice before I walk up to him and introduce myself.

"He isn't talking that much yet, but he will get there," Nancy adds.

I sit and play with him a little bit and when Nancy asks us to go back to her office, Thomas, the older boy points to Max and says "Home?"

"I think we have the answer then," Nancy says. "Well, let's get you guys home then."

EPILOGUE

Samantha

THREE YEARS LATER

"Mommy!" Thomas yells from his room. I go running to him and see that Max, Ethan, and Thomas are all wrestling on the floor. I lean against the door jam and watch my boys play. Max peeks over his shoulder and winks at me.

I watch them play for a while before Max grabs a hold of my ankle and pulls me down to play with them. We all laugh and roll around until our bellies start to hurt.

After the boys are in bed, Max packs his bag to go back to work for a couple of days. He looks over at me and just watches me for a moment. I toss my pillow at him playfully. "What you weirdo?"

"Thank you."

"For what?" I ask.

"Everything. Sammy, you are my everything and you are my salvation."

THE END

Did you enjoy Salvation?

Please take a moment and leave a review on Amazon and Goodreads. I would love to hear your thoughts.

CONTINUE READING FOR A SNEAK PEEK OF INNOCENCE

The story of Allison and Lincoln

Coming December 2020

ALLISON

I walk out of my bar exam, nervous and excited all at the same time. My future can finally begin. Now that both my friends and roommates have moved out and are married, school is over, my exams are over, I can finally be whoever I am meant to be. I just don't know who that is yet.

Lincoln leans up against his car when I walk out of the testing center. I feel the butterflies in my stomach and the knots in my throat tighten. His light brown hair blows in the slight breeze, the wind brings a whiff of his cologne to me and I get goosebumps on my arms. He watches me walk towards him and I see him look me up and down.

He is forbidden though. I would not be the only woman in his life.

LINCOLN

I have my reservations about asking Ally out. I mentally go through my checklist again.

One: She is busy.

Two: I'm busy.

Three: It would be clique for me to date her considering our best friends just got married.

Four: Grace always comes first.

Five: Ally and Grace haven't even really met.

Six: Technically, I am still married.

ACKNOWLEDGMENTS

There is no right order to put these in because you all are important.

Thank you to my family for supporting me and reminding me that I can do this.

William, my dearest husband, thank you for being a sounding board and just nodding your head when I ramble on and on.

Thank you to my best friend and alpha reader, Jenn.

ABOUT THE AUTHOR

Lover of everything books
Born and raised Oregonian.

Billie resides in her home state of Oregon and spends most of her time going to college, reading, writing, and other things normal people try and do.

Ever since she was a young girl, she knew that books would also be a part of her life. Being able to tell stories from her point of view and hope that someone else will fall in love with her characters and their stories as much as she does is all she can ask for.

Want to interact with Billie?

Check out her website and signup for her newsletter at
billieparsons.com

Follow her on Instagram @billieparsons_author

Join her Facebook Reader Group: Billie's Book Babes

Or like her author page on Facebook: Billie Parsons Innocently Romantic @billieparsonsauthor

ALSO BY BILLIE PARSONS

BRADSHAW BROTHERS SERIES

Fragile (Book One)

Salvation (Book Two)

Innocence *(Coming Soon)*

KISS IT SERIES

Kiss of Tomorrow (Prequel)

BOXED SETS AND COLLECTIONS

Locked & Loved: An Isolated Romance Collection